I0680440

Time Will Tell

Michele Doucette

Time Will Tell

Copyright © 2012 by Michele Doucette, St. Clair Publications

All rights reserved. No part of this publication may be reproduced or transmitted in any form or by any means, electronic or mechanical, including photocopying, recording, or by any information storage and retrieval system, without written permission from the author.

ISBN 978-1-935786-34-4

Printed in the United States of America by

St. Clair Publications

PO Box 726

McMinnville, TN   37111-0726

http://stclairpublications.com/

Table of Contents

Dedication

To the many authors, orators and writers, from all walks of life, who continue to inspire me with their compositions, reflections, thoughts and words; may they also continue to remain steadfast to the truth of whom they really are.

To the Cathars of the past, a peaceable and loving people with whom I resonate, most strongly. It may well be that I lived, thusly, in a time, such as this; long gone by.

As always, my husband, Albert; after close to 27 years of dedication to each other, he remains my own special hero.

Acknowledgments

A good writer is someone who writes what they know.

A good writer is someone who writes from the heart.

A good writer is someone who writes with passion.

I do my utmost to adhere to all three noteworthy components.

There are several individuals to whom I owe special acknowledgment, namely:

[1] Shaun George, of New Minas, Nova Scotia, for granting me the privilege of using his photograph, *Portal to the Past*, located on page 40.

You may view his online Flickr photostream at http://www.flickr.com/photos/23641763@N08/

[2] Crooked Arrow Jackson, of Flagstaff, Arizona, for answering questions about the spirit world.

[3] Rolf Müller, for granting me the privilege of using his photograph, *Cathar Dove*, a close-up feature on the monument to the Cathars, located in Minerve, France, as the inside front cover image.

You may view his online Flickr photostream at http://www.flickr.com/photos/gripspix/

[4] William Gunderson, for so inspiring me with his words, that I felt the need to weave them into Chapter 3. It is my hope that many readers will also want to explore his enlightening words at http://www.williamgunderson.com/

Michaela Callaghan had finally discovered her passion; namely, Metaphysics. Her escalating interest in the nature of being, the soul, and existence in time, space and causality, seemed to truly bridge the mystical gap between science and faith; a topic which had long perplexed her.

Completely enthralled with the subject matter, she felt intrinsically driven to complete the *Metaphysical Spirituality* studies program through the American Institute of Holistic Theology, becoming a licensed Metaphysician immediately after acquiring her Doctorate.

So, too, had her dream of finally opening, and operating, an Alternative Health Center, the *All Seeing Eye*, become a reality.

In the course of her studies, she had learned that a Metaphysician is someone who is able to make changes in the physical world through *meta*-physical principles, meaning that they make use of the principles of mind (and beyond) to create powerful and lasting change in their own lives; henceforth, so, too, would they be able to instruct and guide prospective clients in the same manner.

While her upbringing within the Roman Catholic Church had focused on the personage of Jesus, Michaela had been taught next to nothing about his teachings. She had since come to discover, and understand, that Jesus had been both a master Metaphysician as well as a great teacher of metaphysical principles.

It was now so easy to see that his ministry had been one that was based on positive thinking, love, harmlessness, brotherhood and the healing of body, mind and soul.

How different she now felt about Jesus, knowing that man is seen as creator, within the metaphysical realm, due to the fact that it is the mind that controls (creates) each individual reality; meaning that *if you think it, it is so.*

This also means that if one exudes positive thinking, so, too, will increased positivity manifest in their life.

Michaela had also become enlightened to the fact that life, as we know it, is comprised of energy, that energy is held together to create matter (which also includes the physical body), and that matter is energy condensed to a slow vibration because everything is vibration (meaning energy in motion).

"With energy always having existed in some form or another, this means that energy can never be destroyed; instead, it merely transforms into another type of energy."

Finally, she had alighted on a tangible piece of scientific evidence that could give rise to the truth behind the belief in the transmigration of souls; evidence further dictating reincarnation to be both spiritual and physical reality.

Karma, a Sanskrit term, is generally affiliated with the concept of reincarnation. Michaela had since learned that the term karma (meaning action or deed) could also be used to express the scientific law of cause and effect (which, according to Metaphysicians, is also one of the laws of the universe).

By way of a further explanation, energy, as a force, consists of both positive and negative components, each of which acts upon the other to cause a vibration. Without these two opposing forces, there would be no life.

"What this essentially means," she would tell her clients, "is that the totality of life acts (cause) and reacts (effect) because of this pull.

"As you and I create our reality from these two forces, we do our best to try and reach a balance within each lifetime; this shows us how the life principle law of sowing (the seed) and reaping (the harvest) becomes both a scientific and spiritual law, called Karma.

"Knowing that negative karma weighs the soul down and hampers one's personal evolution, it becomes the goal of every soul to enter into its next incarnation with as little negative karma as possible."

Michaela was not surprised to learn that thoughts like fear, greed, hatred, revenge, jealousy, anxiety and frustration are referred to as seeds of disease; a fact that she took the time to share with every client.

"When the body is at *ease* (as in mental, emotional, and spiritual harmony), so, too, is it healthy. By comparison, when the body is at *dis-ease* (meaning mental, emotional, and spiritual disharmony), illness follows.

"In living metaphysical principles, it is through the awareness of personal thoughts that every individual comes to discover that they are not a victim of circumstance. Instead, each comes to fully embrace, and acknowledge, that *life actually follows a pattern according to conscious, and subconscious, thoughts.* Becoming consciously aware of this thinking process, therefore, is a fundamental principle of metaphysics."

It was through further independent study, that Michaela came to discover Parmenides, an early 5th century Greek philosopher, and founder of the Eleatic school of philosophy, who was among the first to propose two differing views of reality (courtesy of a poem, entitled *On Nature*, his only known work that remains).

She found herself quite captivated with the journey of a young man, from darkness to light, as highlighted within the poem; likewise for the two differing views of reality that were cleverly expressed.

"The section called *the Way of Truth* discusses what is real, while the section called *the Way of Opinion* discusses that which is illusionary.

"There are many twenty-first century comparisons that we can draw between these fifth century words, especially as Parmenides shares that there are but two methods of inquiry; namely, that which *is* and that which *is not*.

"Heavily debated since his time, these words have been taken to mean that existence is timeless and eternal, indestructible and unchanging, whereas it becomes in the world of appearances that one's sensory faculties generally lead to conceptions that are both false and deceitful; hence, both the duality, as well as the illusion, that exists in the world of which we live; none other than the world of appearances."

Of course, this early proponent of duality led Michaela to many other thinkers of duality, including those who also spoke of nonduality.

"In summation," she would say, "truth cannot be known through sensory perception for the simple reason that *the perception* (appearance) *of things is deceptive.* What exists, therefore, must always exist; this is what Parmenides is saying."

Having experienced both the effects of positive thinking, as well as the law of attraction, so, too, was she anxious to share the benefits of these metaphysical principles with others. It had also been through the course of her studies that she had come to know, and understand, that it is the metaphysical mind that demonstrates the ability to heal the body, to create or deny peace, and to bring one into conscious awareness; the very same beliefs as held true by Jesus.

In learning about Edgar Cayce, the man who has come to be known as the *sleeping prophet,* a term that made perfect sense when you discovered that his system of metaphysical thought and healing revelations came while he was in a trance, she had come across a book called <u>The Reincarnation of Edgar Cayce</u> by Wynn Free; a book that details a most intriguing connection between Edgar Cayce and David Wilcock.

http://www.bbsradio.com/bbc/wynn_free/wynn_free.shtml

What Michaela found so utterly fascinating was how closely young Edgar Cayce (photo on the left) also resembled young David Wilcock (photo on the right).

"When we are speaking about reincarnation, there exists documented evidence to say that personality traits, personal

11

preferences, habits and behavior seem to carry over from one lifetime to another. In addition, individuals also seem to bear a facial resemblance to whom they were before. As well, the new bodies often have visible birthmarks in areas where the alleged self had been wounded."

In referencing websites, as well as books, whereby such information exists, and cannot be disputed, she found that a great many people were completely astounded to discover the physicality of the immortality of the human soul.

Trained as a Past Life Regressionist, so, too, was she able to offer an overview of past-life theory before engaging in past-life regression as a form of awakening, healing, and spiritual renewal.

In having experienced, firsthand, the healing power of the Labyrinth, at the Chartres Cathedral in France, Michaela had taken it upon herself to include a permanent, terra cotta and turquoise granite resin, Chartres Cathedral style labyrinth (situated outdoors) as part of the initial plans for the center.

Whenever the weather was not conducive to walking the outside labyrinth, she felt renewed in knowing that she could still offer the same experience to her clients, for she had also elected to have a much smaller, Chartres Cathedral style, labyrinth painted on the floor of the Meditation room.

"The labyrinth has been walked since ancient times," Michaela would always begin, as a means of introduction.

"As a sacred tool, the labyrinth is used for reflection, meditation, and realignment with one's inner being, all of which result in a deeper knowledge of the inner self. Unlike a maze, the labyrinth has only one path; the way in is also the way out.

"In combining the imagery of the circle together with the spiral, we end up with a meandering, but purposeful path. In this way, the labyrinth becomes a metaphor for the journey of life, the journey to your deepest self, whereby you grow in compassion and are, therefore, able to respond to the world with increased clarity and wisdom. In this way, you emerge with a clearer understanding of who you really are; the ultimate journey of each individual."

Some of Michaela's most well attended workshops were those based on how to construct a simple outdoor labyrinth.

Realignment with one's inner being results in personal transformation. Knowing that each individual is also able to demonstrate an ability to harness the power of the unconscious mind in order to reach their spiritual potential, as she, herself, had proven (through creative visualization, Mind Movies and affirmations), so, too, did she offer related workshops.

It was through her daily Meditation regimen that she had also learned the importance of exploring mindfulness as a method for integration, wholeness, and self-realization, preferring to meditate within the confines of her copper pyramid.

It is known that the pyramid activates the energies of both the pineal and pituitary glands. Users have been noted to experience balance, relaxation, tranquility, well-being, and, in some instances, the reduction of headaches.

Further independent study, pertaining to the pyramid research conducted by the Russian National Academy of Sciences, had alerted her to the knowledge that the energy field within the pyramid appears to act as a type of vortex, the proven benefits of which are completely astounding.

"You can use copper pyramids to charge your crystals and stones. Some people use pyramids to imbue their drinking water with negative ions, which have a most positive effect. Negative ions are naturally found in all of the different places that make us feel good after we have visited them: the beach, the mountains, the country and forests, as well as any areas that are situated near waterfalls.

"Negative ions help to reproduce and repair the cells within our bodies. Not only are they transmitted into the body through the air, but they are also circulated by the blood. Too many positive ions (which are mainly the result of air pollution) can cause depression, and, ultimately, illnesses; thus, negative ions have an extremely beneficial effect on the body.

"Pyramids generate negative ions. In addition, they are believed to have a balancing effect on the electromagnetic field of the body. This effect is further enhanced if the materials used are either gold or copper.

"Once these negative ions reach our bloodstream, it is believed that they produce biochemical reactions that increase levels of the mood chemical serotonin, which further helps to alleviate depression, relieve stress, and boost our daytime energy.

"We know that copper is a good conductor of electricity. It is also believed that copper serves as a conductor of the subtle energies, facilitating the direction and flow of that energy, which provides for a harmonic connection between the physical and astral bodies. This is why you will find a copper pyramid, for meditative purposes, in the Healing room."

Michaela was quite familiar with Eastern thought in reference to the chakra system; a system that can be opened, cleared and balanced for spiritual, psychological, and physical healing.

Attempting to explain the etheric body system to her clients was always a challenge; one that she willingly embraced, all in an effort to help them understand what they could do for themselves.

In seeing the power of the breath as being the first real miracle, she began every client session in the same manner, by asking that each individual take a few moments to contemplate, and truly appreciate, the wonder of breathing; a time whereby each would simply breathe in through their nostrils and out through their mouths, with eyes closed.

"In truth, we must all become *more mindful* of this exquisite gift, a gift beyond measure, a gift that many have a tendency to take completely for granted.

"Without attempting to achieve transcended awareness, you can experience a *change in consciousness* when you take five to ten minutes, per day, to concentrate solely on the process of breathing."

Michaela would explain that whenever she was feeling uptight, anxious or upset about something, she would retreat to a space whereby she would focus only on her breathing; a technique that very much served to relax her, thereby allowing her to see things from a different perspective.

"Life is a sacred journey. So, too, is it a journey that embraces change, growth, discovery, movement and transformation."

Thoroughly impressed with the American Institute of Holistic Theology, she was also eager to complete their *Healtheology* program.

Immediately after receiving her Doctorate in Healtheology, she was able to become nationally board certified by the American Association of Drugless Practitioners as well as the American Holistic Health Alliance.

Healtheology is a field of study that references a theological science of health, meaning that health and theology have a common ground.

So, too, is it a study that delves into such components as therapeutic massage, reflexology, aromatherapy, light therapy, music therapy, color therapy, vision therapy, therapeutic nutrition, juicing and nutrition, basic macrobiotics, somatic techniques, polarity healing, understanding dreams, development of the mind, exploring hypnosis, spontaneous healing, spirituality and personal transformation, shamanic journeys, crystals and gemstones, herbology, homeopathy, Ayurveda, vibrational healing, therapeutic prayer, psychic healing and transpersonal psychology.

In her spare time, Michaela also found herself working her way through the *Alternate Spiritual Traditions* program of study as well, with topics related to Angels, intuitive and psychic abilities, past-life regression, Buddhism, karma, astrology, paranormal phenomena, Taoism, feng shui, numerology, ancient tools (I-Ching, tarot, runes), near-death experiences (NDEs), handwriting analysis, extraterrestrial theories of Zecharia Sitchin, trance, prayer, the rave culture, shamanism, meditation and out-of-body experiences (OBEs).

Chapter 2

In wanting to help others create a more positive, responsible, responsive and objective lifestyle, Dr. Mike realized the importance of conducting introductory workshops on Metaphysics, with material that could then be used as an expansion for individual growth and study.

Workshop Notes

Meta means *after* or *beyond* and physics means *matter*, *material things* or the *physical*. Metaphysics, then, literally pertains to the study of the true nature of reality (the spiritual force behind physicality). It was Aristotle who first coined the phrase; it was also Aristotle who said that *thoughts are the creative elements within us that make our life what it is*.

The principles of metaphysics are based on the perception that we are not simply physical bodies. There is also a spiritual basis to our physical existence, for we are a coming together of Universal Mind (shared spiritual consciousness) with Physical Mind (physical matter).

In the noteworthy words of Pierre Teilhard de Chardin, a French philosopher and Jesuit priest, who trained as both a paleontologist as well as a geologist, as penned in his 1955 publication, Le Phénomène Humain [1] ...

We are not human beings having a spiritual experience; we are spiritual beings having a human experience.

In essence, this means that we are not human beings on a spiritual journey.

Rather, we are spiritual beings on a journey into *what it means* to be human.

These words, very much echo the beliefs of a metaphysician.

So, too, were these words of his taken from the same publication ... **A universal love is not only psychologically possible; it is the only complete and final way in which we are able to love.**

---

[1] http://www.archive.org/details/phenomenon-of-man-pierre-teilhard-de-chardin.pdf

Metaphysics, then, is a system that allows us to fully integrate our spiritual expression with the physical and mental aspects of life. Interestingly, it was Carl Jung who said *modern man is in search of his soul.*

Applied metaphysics simply implies that one is living their life in accordance with metaphysical principles (a spiritual, moral and ethical practice that can lead to better results in any area of life they choose).

In essence, all forms of metaphysical practice, when applied properly, will operate from the perspective of simultaneous cause and effect; a process that eliminates the illusion of separateness because the student becomes one with the subject of their attention.

This simply means that you give meaning, and form, to that which you experience; hence, it exists.

While one of the principles of metaphysics is to set goals, it is equally as imperative that you see yourself achieving these goals *in your mind first.*

The things that you wish to manifest in your life will come into your experience when you learn, and choose, to give them both meaning as well as form (with vision boards and Mind Movies being fine examples).

Meditation is one of the central tenets for developing the benefits of spiritual and metaphysical wisdom. Taking the time to focus on love and peace, empathy and compassion (all in keeping with a heart-based consciousness), while meditating, also increases its overall effectiveness.

Science has already proven that meditation puts the mind in a more relaxed, productive, and effective state that releases stress, thereby leading to a significantly beneficial effect upon one's health and relationships; all of which leads to increased inner peace.

In accordance with this wisdom, first and foremost, you must acknowledge that *you are the creator of your reality*. Knowing that you are both script writer and director of your life, there is nothing outside of yourself that can control you (meaning your actions, thoughts, words and deeds); hence, you are *never* a victim.

Likewise, you are always free to choose whatever actions you desire; nothing ever interferes with that choice. It only becomes in the acting upon your decisions that you experience the natural consequences of them, whatever that may be.

It is equally as important to remember that when you make the choice not to act, not to do something, and/or to remain detached (which can work out to be both positive as well as negative), that, too, is also a choice.

In essence, *you are totally responsible for you*; there is no one else to blame.

If ever you appeared to be a victim, it was because you gave your power away to someone (or something) outside of yourself, refusing to take responsibility.

We are both a unified consciousness as well an individuated extension of the Divine; as a result, love is our intrinsic nature, our inherent being.

Knowing that all of creation has been derived from love, so, too, is creation perfect.

As we all make more of a conscious effort to create an increase in positive thoughts (while also living this truth), this is what serves to create a more peaceful world.

Like attracts like, meaning love and positivity can only attract more of the same.

The Law of Attraction, simply put, means that *you will get more of that which you think about and dwell upon*, so guard your thoughts most carefully.

As Anastasia of the Siberian tiaga has stated throughout the Ringing Cedars series, Man is Creator. In keeping, so, too, is God Creator. Likewise, God is thought; henceforth, thought is also Creator.

After all, was not the beginning stated as being the Word? What was the Word, then, if not thought?

Man creates his (her) reality through thought. It all comes down to what does Man wish to create, does it not?

In essence, then, *thought is the beginning of all creation*, meaning that *you create with your thoughts*.

We become what we think. We become what we feel. We become what we believe.

With free will to think anything that you choose, it is the *intent* (emotion) *placed behind the thought* that allows the thought to manifest as creation.

Only you can choose how you feel about your experience(s). Only you can change your thoughts, choosing anew.

By changing your thoughts, you change your life experience(s).

Does not this equate to personal empowerment?

The universe can only respond to choices, as made by you. As you change your thoughts, so, too, do you change your choices; likewise for your life, however minor it may seem.

Thought is energy and energy always follows thought. In keeping, matter follows energy.

This means that negative experiences always follow negative perceptions; likewise, positive experiences will always follow positive perceptions.

Positive thinking and experiencing does not allow for the accepting of defeat, or limitation, in either one's thinking or their achievements.

If you embrace love, peace, unison and truth, feeling and living (vibrating) such throughout the entirety of your being, you will experience people (as well as places, things or events) that emit these corresponding vibrations.

If, on the other hand, all you experience in your outer world is disharmony, aggression, hate, separation and falsehood, so, too, will you experience people (as well as places, things or events) that match these same resonance levels.

Unfortunately, it is far easier to look at the negative (darker) side of life than the positive (creative).

Research has stated that while our lives are governed by our subconscious mind (that part of ourselves that shapes (controls) at least 95% of the decisions that we make), we are only conscious of about 5% of our cognitive activity.

This means, in essence, that most of our decisions, actions and behavior, depend on the 95% of brain activity that goes beyond our conscious awareness.

What is even more frightening is the fact that approximately 70% of our thoughts are negative, meaning that if we think negative thoughts, throughout most of the day, thoughts that we may not even be aware of, our vibrations will continue to emanate at a low level.

How, then, can one make the necessary shift in consciousness? The solution lies in the re-programming of the subconscious mind. There are many tools that can be used, such as Affirmations, Creative Visualization (as in both vision boards as well as Mind Movies), Hypnotherapy, Repatterning Hypnosis, Neuro Hypnotic Repatterning and NLP (Neuro Linguistic Programming), to mention a few.

If applied properly, metaphysics serves to change that inner feeling of *I'm not good enough* or *I'm not worthy enough* or *I haven't got the necessary skills for the job that I want* to a new realization of one's own Beingness (which truly encompasses who, and what, you really are, where you came from and what you are ultimately here to do).

By choosing to change your thinking (which is the cause), you create new experiences in your life (which, thereby, become the effect); hence, one's thoughts are tangible, are they not?

As thoughts change, in reference to one's truth, in reference to one's inner wisdom, so, too, is one's perception altered.

As you can see, while metaphysics places a strong emphasis on the mind, in retrospect, it is very much concerned with the soul essence of a person.

If one is also being completely honest, one can readily acknowledge that our minds have been brainwashed (conditioned) by significant societal forces (religion, education, politics, culture, parental guidance).

Metaphysics demonstrates that we can be free of these instilled and inherited belief systems, learning to separate the self from those things that the society places upon the self.

As a result, metaphysical principles enable one to look at situations with more clarity and objectivity. This is not something that happens instantaneously, nor does it happen overnight; metaphysics is a life-long discipline that takes years.

In experiencing and applying metaphysical principles, you gradually (and quite gently, at that) learn to alter your thinking, your emotions, your lifestyle; thereafter, it can be said that you have become a metaphysician.

One must start by accepting certain principles and allowing them to work first in the mind. Once each principle is understood, the spiritual aspect of the mind works with the physical body, creating a different response from before. Indeed, it is also a mental process that includes both your emotions and passions.

Most are familiar with the saying that *the outer world is your mirror*, always *reflecting yourself back to you*. This simply means that your outer world is a direct reflection of your inner world.

When you come to fully understand this principle, you become more mindful about judging and criticizing others, for, in effect, you are judging and criticizing yourself.

You see, everything comes back to self. In *learning to act as compared to react*, one is able to create a much better world for themselves (and others).

Total commitment to change and growth (because all change leads to growth), as well as to the empowerment of one's Beingness, can be likened to the seed that must be planted deep within; one that is nurtured through mental discipline and devotion to this new path, until it becomes a tangible one, able to live and breathe inside you in the most naturalistic of ways.

As long as you continue to react to outer circumstances, you will respond in a negative fashion. If you elect, instead, to remain self-contained and uninfluenced by outside forces, you are able to set the tone for your own day to day living in the now.

It becomes in living, thinking and acting from the heart that one can say they are living a fully integrated life; our key purpose being to become a true spiritual individual, much like Christ (who lived the inner, pure, real Self).

It is of the utmost importance that each individual, in the accepting of who they really are, is able to transform themselves into the inner Christ that lives within.

I believe the purpose of life is to be happy.

We are here to focus on what creates happiness, joy and passion in our lives.

One must be ready, able and willing to walk this path; a path that may take more than one lifetime.

We have to understand that love is all that exists. Given that we are extensions of the Divine, love is our intrinsic nature.

So, too, are we a unified consciousness. Unfortunately, this has not been the upbringing of most of us.

This is why metaphysics can easily be deemed an intellectual exercise whereby [1] the mind is reshaped and disciplined, [2] correct thinking (meaning positivity, objectivity and positive detachment) is encouraged, and [3] pure spiritual thinking (existing from the heart) is formed.

In effect, it is courtesy of this necessary marriage of mind (ego) and soul (heart) that further enables each person to bring about essential changes within the self as well as within his (her) environment (world).

In truth, this gives one much to ponder, does it not?

Chapter 3

When an individual comes to the realization that they are not living a fulfilled life and/or not experiencing joy in living, they want answers, as well as change. So, too, was this the experience of Dr. Mike.

As they continue to seek answers, their Inner Wisdom *begins to guide them to information that reveals to them the power within their very being* … [a power that] *is connected to an infinite source beyond their own physical brain and body.* [2]

Ultimately, Dr. Mike was also quick to recognize that she needed to take each client to this very same starting point; the realization that total power is to be found within.

"Many are familiar with the saying, *when the student is ready, the teacher will appear.* In truth, all are both student as well as teacher.

---

[2] http://www.williamgunderson.com/content/view/42/71/

"When properly attuned to one's intuition, synchronistic signs can also *come in the form of an overheard comment or a glance at a discarded newspaper or a book that catches one's attention while browsing in a bookstore or library,* [3] all of which are answers that have been provided by the universe. It is up each individual, therefore, to recognize these signs as individualized responses."

Dr. Mike knew that the journey to awareness began the moment that one was able to make the decision to follow where these signs might lead. She would often reference that it was in following this yellow brick road to inner wisdom, so to speak, that the student would come to discover that following one source would usually lead to another and another and another; hence, it was not uncommon for the individual to *begin meandering about a seemingly endless flow of subtopics within the broad field of metaphysics and mysticism, getting off the main path and taking many side trips"* [4]

---

[3] http://www.williamgunderson.com/content/view/42/71/
[4] Ibid.

In the confusion that would often follow, she was able to respond by saying that it was important to recognize that their inner (higher) guidance had not forsaken them; instead, it was more like they were *exploring, without asking specific enough questions.* [5]

Likewise, it was as equally attributable to the fact that they had *not yet learned to recognize, and, thus, be able to heed the directions of their inner voices.* [6]

"It must also be remembered that *each journey is as unique as the individual.*

"You can rest assured, however, that once the journey to merge the ego with the heart, eventually culminating in a heart-based conscious existence, has begun, there really is no turning back to the previous ways of the conventional wisdom of the world; if, indeed, it can be considered wisdom in its truest sense, given that the answers sought can never be found outside of one's being.

---

[5] http://www.williamgunderson.com/content/view/42/71/
[6] Ibid.

"This is why you must always be cautious when choosing a teacher (to follow) or a group (to join). It is far more important that you follow your intuition; that you learn to relax, trusting in your Inner Guidance.

"A good teacher, should one come along, exists only to guide the student towards discovering the truths that already exist within; reminding the student that they, too, have equal access to universal wisdom. In truth, all need only to learn how to do so.

"As you learns to surrender the limiting beliefs of the ego to the all-encompassing love of the heart, you enter into the metamorphosis (transformation) phase; a phase whereby [1] you have made the decision to live an empowered life (meaning that you have taken back your power), [2] you want to have full control over your experience, [3] you want to create the conditions of your life in total congruency with your desires (which means you are now creating with conscious intent as opposed to creating by default), [4] you are discovering that resistance interferes with peace of mind, [5] you want to be able to go with the flow (to live, act and exist in the now), an action that serves to create increased peace of mind, and [6] you resonate more with your spiritual self, as compared to the human ego self, becoming, and living, the God(dess) within (both in word and deed)."

Dr. Mike was always quick to highlight that this transcendental awareness journey begins the moment one realizes that they wish to let go of the fear-based beliefs that merely serve to keep one enslaved within the limitation mode of thinking and existing; a personal reality that is made up of the inherited belief system(s) as held by the individual.

"In the knowingness (and acknowledgement) that you create your reality, such triggers the ultimate realization; meaning, of course, that you are the only one who has the power to release yourself from this self imposed bondage.

"There is nothing that exists outside of you that has any power over you, unless you choose to give it away; so, too, upon realizing the happenings of the past, must you also choose to take it back, for therein lies increased peace of mind."

Chapter 4

In direct association with her studies as a Past-Life Regressionist, Dr. Mike was driven to purchase a large, hand carved, Calavera Stone crystal skull. Calavera is a stone that is mined in Wyoming, but on a very limited basis.

She had also learned, from eBay store owner, Ravenia Youngman, [7] that this Calavera Stone was also referenced as the *Stone of Primal Memories*.

In meditating with this amazingly beautiful druzy skull, she had been able to access the far reaches of one of her soul's memories; that of having lived as a Cathar healer and herbalist in Béziers, France, during the time of the Albigensian Crusades.

According to some Cathars, "the purpose of man's life on Earth was to transcend matter; perpetually renouncing anything connected with the principle of power and thereby attaining union with the principle of love. According to

---

[7] http://stores.ebay.ca/Crystal-Skull-Head-Quarters

others, man's purpose was to reclaim or redeem matter, spiritualizing and transforming it." [8] Dr. Mike would soon come to better understand both aspects.

Portal from the Past

© Shaun R. George

---

[8] http://www.serenitytravels.com/cathar_missions.html

Chapter 5

Location: Château de Foix, Languedoc, southern France

Time: July 22, 1195

Raymond Roger, the son and successor of Roger Bernard I and Cécile Trencavel, was the fifth count of Foix from the House of Foix; famed for his generalship and chivalry, he prided himself on fidelity.

On this particular occasion, the birth of his second illegitimate child, he vowed, at age forty-three, there would be no more children, legitimate or otherwise.

With the Kingdom of Jerusalem having been captured by Saladin in 1187, such began the Third Crusade. Raymond Roger had accompanied King Philippe II Augustus to Palestine, leaving Vézelay on July 1, 1190, part of the French army which consisted of six hundred fifty knights, one thousand three hundred horses and one thousand three hundred squires, to recover the Holy City.

At first the French and English crusaders traveled together, but the armies split at Lyon. King Richard I of England, dubbed Richard the Lionhearted because of his reputation as a great military leader and warrior, decided to travel the remainder of the distance by sea, while Philippe took the overland route through the Alps to Genoa.

Reunited in Messina, Italy, they wintered together. It was on March 30, 1191, that the French set sail for the Holy Land, arriving on April 20, with a Genoese fleet under the command of Simone Doria. Marching to Acre, Philippe began to construct large siege equipment, like the trebuchet, before the arrival of Richard on June 8. [9]

The siege machines [10] continued to break holes in the walls of Acre; in keeping, every new breach led to yet another attack by Saladin's army, giving the garrison at Acre time to repair the damages.

---

[9] Rickard, Jim. (12 November 2001), *Siege of Acre, August 1189 to July 12, 1191,* accessed on December 11, 2011 at
http://www.historyofwar.org/articles/battles_acre.html
[10] http://www.strangecosmos.com/content/item/169848.html

Eventually, however, the long siege of Acre, first begun in August 1189, was won by the Christian crusaders on July 12, 1191, with Raymond Roger earning several distinguished honors while there.

Hugh III, Duke of Burgundy, had also traveled to the Holy Land with Philippe. Having fought alongside Richard, he quickly became a most trusted ally of the English king. Upon Philippe's return to France on July 31, 1191, it was Hugh who he left in charge of the French troops: 10,000 men remaining in Outremer.

Raymond Roger arrived home in March 1193, following the end of the Third Crusade in October 1192.

Accustomed to the sights, sounds and smells of battle that were forever thereafter etched in one's psychc, he found that he was unable to endure the harsh rigors associated with birthing.

Mon dieu ... how do our women endure this, day after day; they are surely the stronger of the sexes, he thought, as he mopped his sweaty brow for what seemed the hundredth time.

Positioned in front of the fireplace, nestled inside the Great Hall, sitting in his special chair had always brought comfort and solace, but not this day; his mind was a tormented lot.

He had come back from the Holy Land a changed man.

Having married Philippa of Montcada, in 1189, at the age of thirty-seven, he'd already fathered one illegitimate child many years prior. Less than a year into their marriage, he was off to the Holy Land.

Roger Bernard II, born January 1194, the apple of his eye, had just turned sixteen months old.

Here he sat, in the wee hours of July 22, 1195, still appalled at having fathered yet another illegitimate child, when Philippa, herself, had just given birth to their second child, a daughter, a few months earlier, named after his mother, Cécile Trencavel of Béziers; Cécile Trencavel was the daughter of Raymond I Trencavel, an important and noble family in the Languedoc.

Keeping to himself, in the darkest of spaces, he was profoundly relieved when the child was delivered safely by the midwife. Mere moments later, however, he was consumed by both agony as well as guilt upon learning that Isabeau, the child's mother, had not survived the birth.

The midwife, present at the birth of Isabeau de Foix, so named in honor of her mother, foretold that she was the healer, long awaited by the Cathari. It was also shared that she would have the gift of sight, able to see the fae folk of the forest and meadows.

It was for this very reason that she would be sent to Béziers, to apprentice under a Cathari healer and herbalist, when she became of age. In the meantime, however, it was decided that Esclarmonde de Foix, sister to Raymond Roger, a follower of the Cathar faith, would raise Isabeau under her roof.

Between sixteen month old Roger Bernard and two month old Cécile, Philippa already had enough to contend with.

Château de Foix

http://fr.wikipedia.org/wiki/Fichier:Ch%C3%A2teau_de_Fo
ix_Lespinet.JPG

Château de Foix, built atop an older 7th century fortification which dominated the town, provided control over the whole of the upper valley, holding its own, situated like an eagle's nest, a citadel of importance and impregnability, in the Languedoc; an area, known previously as Septimania, that was "culturally and politically separate from northern France and the central royal government." [11]

Of Merovingian stock, Roger I of Carcassonne, also known as Roger II of Comminges the Elder, was the Count of Carcassonne, Couserans and Comminges.

In 1002, the castle "figured in the testament of Roger, the first count of Carcassonne, who bequeathed it to his eldest son Bernard Roger," [12] the first to use the title Comte (Count) de Foix. The house of Foix was of Iberian origin,

---

[11] http://en.wikipedia.org/wiki/Septimania
[12]
http://www.castlesandmanorhouses.com/catharcastles/foix.php?key=fo ix

going "all the way back to Adcantuan who had fought against Caesar." [13]

From there the Château passed to [1] Roger I, second son of Bernard Roger, who never married; [2] Pierre Bernard, third son of Bernard Roger; [3] Roger II, eldest son of Pierre Bernard; [4] Roger III, eldest son of Roger II, [5] Roger Bernard I, only son of Roger III, and [6] Raymond Roger, second son of Roger Bernard I, and great, great, great grandson of Bernard Roger.

The Languedoc had much in common with Byzantium, in that each held knowledge and learning in high esteem; likewise, the nobility were both literate and literary.

In a culture that was advanced for its time, "the high concentration of Jews and Muslims among the population bears silent testimony to an unusual degree of religious tolerance ... an overlapping of the cultures and the Muslim

---

[13]

http://www.rosicrucian.org/publications/digest/digest2_2011/04_web/09_hbernard/09_hbernard_112311.pdf

influence that gave rise to the South's artistic and scientific achievements." [14]

Historically, the area of the Languedoc was referred to as the county of Toulouse. The hereditary Counts of Toulouse "ruled the city of Toulouse and its surrounding county from the late 9th century until 1270. The counts and other family members were also, at various times, Counts of Quercy, Rouergue, Albi, and Nîmes, and Margraves of Gothia and Provence." [15]

As a successor state for the Visigothic Kingdom, "Toulouse, along with Aquitania and Languedoc (but not Gascony), inherited the Visigothic Law and Roman Law which had combined to allow women more rights than their contemporaries would enjoy until the 20th century. Women could inherit land and title and manage it independently from their husbands or male relations, dispose of their

---

[14]

http://www.dhaxem.com/data/handt/The_Great_Esclarmonde_of_the_Cathars.pdf

[15] http://en.wikipedia.org/wiki/Counts_of_Toulouse#cite_ref-Visgothic_Women_0-0

property in legal wills if they had no heirs, and women could represent themselves and bear witness in court by age 14 and arrange for their own marriages by age 20. As a consequence, male-preference primogeniture [a term which meant that the first born would inherit the entire estate, to the exclusion of younger siblings] was the practiced succession law for the nobility." [16] [17] [18]

Catharism first appeared in southern France, the area of the Languedoc, sometime in the years following the First Crusade (1096 to 1099). Featuring both dualistic and Gnostic components, its adherents "quickly became numerous and well organised, electing bishops, collecting funds and distributing money to the poor; but they could not accept that if there was only one God, and if God was the creator, and if God was good, that there should be suffering, illness and death in his world." [19]

---

[16] http://en.wikipedia.org/wiki/Counts_of_Toulouse#cite_ref-Visgothic_Women_0-0
[17] http://en.wikipedia.org/wiki/Visigothic_Code
[18] http://en.wikipedia.org/wiki/Primogeniture
[19] http://bogomiltocathar.devhub.com/blog/588653-templars-and-cathars/

There have been many comparisons between this Church of Love (AMOR) versus the Church of Rome (ROMA).

The Cathars believed that "one object of Earth life was to make over the human body as a worthy vehicle for the light of the Holy Spirit (love). The point was to *know the Grail* not as a cup but *as a process*. Insight into this teaching radiates from the name of the Languedoc [in that] the Cathar priests claimed Jesus preached in the Language of Oc (possibly short for occamy, a corruption of alchemy)", [20] with his teachings leading to enlightenment (as well as the transforming of human blood into the blood of light, also synonymous with the Holy Grail).

The Cathars believed in "a good and an evil principle, the former the creator of the invisible and spiritual universe, the latter the creator of our material world. While most Cathars lived outwardly normal lives, pledging to renounce the evil

---

[20] http://www.bibliotecapleyades.net/esp_autor_whenry04.htm

world on their deathbeds, a few lived the strict life of the *perfecti*." [21]

Firm believers in reincarnation, the Cathars also recognized, and acknowledged, the feminine principle. So, too, did they understand that "knowledge or *gnosis* took precedence over all creeds and dogma." [22]

Forming their own church, in opposition to Rome, they "lived their lives in peace and harmony with nature. Women were held in high esteem, and allowed to preach." [23]

In accordance with Cathari belief, Jesus came to transmit a message; namely, to reveal the truth (as related to our *real* eternal and spiritual essence) and *not* to redeem the sins of all men by his death.

In keeping with classical Gnosticism, Manichaeism and the theology of the Bogomils, the Cathars believed that there existed, within mankind, a spark of divine light, and that this

---

[21] http://bogomiltocathar.devhub.com/blog/588653-templars-and-cathars/
[22] http://www.laughingowl.com/aleta/Knightsandsecret.htm
[23] Ibid.

"light, or spirit, had fallen into captivity within a realm of corruption; identified with the material world."[24]

Liberation from "the realm of limitation and corruption identified with material existence"[25] was, therefore, the goal, with the path to sovereignty first requiring "an awakening to the intrinsic corruption of the medieval *consensus reality*, including its ecclesiastical, dogmatic, and social structures."[26]

Upon becoming cognizant "of the grim existential reality of human existence (the *prison* of matter), the path to spiritual liberation became obvious: matter's enslaving bonds must be broken. This was a step by step process, accomplished in different measures by each individual."[27]

In acknowledging reincarnation, "those who were unable to achieve liberation during their current mortal journey would return later to continue the struggle ... resultant of the fact

---

[24] http://www.book-of-thoth.com/thebook/index.php/Cathars
[25] Ibid.
[26] Ibid.
[27] Ibid.

that not all humans could break the enthralling chains of matter within a single lifetime." [28] This belief further denoted the immortality of the human soul.

Their message was one of love, tolerance, freedom and equality between men and women, and yet they were slaughtered by the Roman Church.

In medieval France, it was this sect of enlightened mystics who "tried to preserve Christ's true message," [29] possibly because they possessed "evidence of a more authentic version of early Christianity ... much more dangerous than a Jewish bloodline: ancient scrolls containing lost teachings of Christ that contradicted the canonical gospels." [30]

Known as *Les Bons Hommes* and *Les Bonnes Femmes*, meaning *the good people*, it was their involvement in helping to fight poverty, as well as their denial of the authority of the church, that are important arguments for some researchers to denote the Cathars "as church reformists

---

[28] http://www.book-of-thoth.com/thebook/index.php/Cathars
[29] http://www.ru.org/spirituality/remembering-the-cathars.html
[30] Ibid.

and mystical Christians who reacted to the riches and despotism in the Roman Church." [31]

Despite the fact that St. Bernard of Clairvaux tried to bring the Cathars back into the orthodox fold of the church, it is worth citing his words ... *No sermons are more thoroughly Christian than theirs, and their morals are pure.*

Philippa, step-mother of Isabeau, loved and admired Esclarmonde, her sister-in-law, quickly following in her footsteps on the perilous path of Catharism.

As a *credente*, like Esclarmonde, she was not expected to adopt the same stringent lifestyle of the *perfecti*.

While their priesthood "was open to both men and women, who practiced herbalism, vegetarianism, celibacy, tolerance, simplicity, and pacifism, [the] Cathar laypeople followed the

---

[31] http://www.et-in-arcadia-ego.com/html/Arcadia0B.php

messages of simplicity and tolerance, but weren't under the strictures that forbade meat, marriage, and sex." [32]

Unable to embrace a life of complete purity, Philippa looked forward to an eventual time, after having acquired some experience in the physical world, when this would also become her calling, her path.

---

[32] Shesso, Renna. (2007) *Math for Mystics: From the Fibonacci Sequence to Luna's Labyrinth to the Golden Section and Other Secrets of Sacred Geometry* (page 74). San Francisco, CA: Weiser Books.

Chapter 7

The town of Foix, it is said, owed its origin to a chapel founded by Charlemagne, thereafter becoming the Abbey of Saint Volusianus in 849 AD.

Surrounded by mountains that harbor many lateral valleys, forests and rivers, and situated on an impressive rock plateau, Château de Foix was an undeniably imposing, and, yet, completely striking structure.

It was here that Raymond Roger was able to watch over the countryside, protected by unbreachable walls.

The placement of the castle was extremely well chosen from a strategy standpoint, dating "from an era of great insecurity, banditry and territorial rivalries. In addition it had to be a commanding presence in the passage through the Pyrenees mountain chain in order to counter invasions." [33]

---

[33] http://www.ariege.com/chateaudefoix/info.html

There was a song that was sung, with lyrics denoting the security of the castle – "*El castels es tant fortz qu'el mezis se defent* ... the castle is so strong it can defend itself." [34]

The "huge rock rising above the confluence of the Ariège and Arget rivers," [35] on which the castle was built, was the "perfect place from which to command the trade routes along the two rivers." [36]

Inhabited in prehistoric times, with a fortress erected in the Merovingian era, Château de Foix was constructed around the year 1000. More than 34 meters high, it was built on a steep slope, supported by impressive flying buttress. While the Château was "defended by two walls with a large barbican (double gate), the town lay at the foot of the rock, protected by the ramparts joining the natural defenses of the two rivers." [37]

---

[34] http://www.ariege.com/chateaudefoix/info.html
[35] http://shadowtheatre13.com/gazetteer.html
[36] Ibid.
[37] Ibid.

The Romance language (as in *to speak in Roman*) of the area, Occitan, or the *langue d'oc*, developed from Vulgar Latin, and was a language that was understood, and celebrated, throughout most of educated Europe.

It was in this very language that troubadours "composed lyric courtly love poems, called *canso*, and traveled to the seigneurial courts reciting their works." [38]

Not simply a patron of the troubadours, Raymond Roger was also a formidable poet himself. A partisan of the Occitan cause, he was referred to "in the popular troubadour romances as Raimond Drut or Raimond the Beloved." [39] So, too, was he also famed for his loyalty and attachment to paratge.

Also a poet, as well as a man of culture, Raymond VI, Count of Toulouse (maternal grandson of King Louis VI and his second wife) was a close relative of Raymond Roger.

---

[38]

http://www.cliffordawright.com/caw/food/entries/display.php/topic_id/21/id/63/

[39] http://shadowtheatre13.com/gazetteer.html

In keeping, Raymond Roger was one of his staunchest allies.

With influences from the bordering countries of Navarre, Aragon, Cataloma (Catalonia) and Barcelona to the south, Gascony to the east, Provence to the west, France to the north, including the entire Mediterranean world to the south, the cuisine of the Languedoc was exceptionally varied.

An area sympathetic to peoples of different nationalities and religious beliefs, as well as one where learning was highly esteemed (based on a significant body of Arabic knowledge, especially in reference to astronomy, astrology, philosophy and medicine, their long lineage dating back through extending through the Egyptians, Greeks, and Essenes), the nobility of the Languedoc quickly grew to appreciate certain Arab flavouring spices, such as saffron and cinnamon.

A simple fava bean stew, often enriched with goose, duck, pork skin, and a simple pork sausage with a distinctive flavour, simmering in a cauldron over an open hearth fire, was an area favorite.

One of the oldest plants under cultivation, fava beans were very popular in Mediterranean cuisine, with a distinct flavor and creamy texture making them a great addition to a wide variety of dishes.

A seasonal bean that could also be dried for winter use, fava beans needed to be shelled and peeled before eating because the outer peel, while edible, had an incredibly woody texture, one that took away from the inner bean.

The harder the cooking water, the better the beans would maintain their shape. Patience was required as the cooking was long, with the fire needing to be adjusted as often as might be necessary.

During the cooking, a film would develop over the stew; culinary folklore instructed that this film be broken seven times in order to make the perfect *cassoulet*.

They also enjoyed a *poularde* made with chicken. On the bottom of a pot, they would cook pork with slices of onion, carrots and a sprig of thyme, to which would be added a small chicken.

Covering the pan, they would allow the chicken to sweat (roast) in a small fire. Turning the chicken every so often, they added white wine and mushroom caps, after a time. This would be left to simmer before covering the chicken with water, allowing it to finish cooking over low heat.

After removing the chicken and fixings, which might also include anything else that was on hand, a gravy would be made from adding butter and flour to the broth.

So, too, might you find a hearty beef stew, or *daube*, simmering over an open hearth. After cutting beef into large pieces, for immediate browning in fat, peeled onions, carrots and leeks (all, of which, had been cut in large chunks), quartered tomatoes, mushrooms, garlic, wine and herbs (thyme, rosemary, bay and sorrel were especially popular) would be added to the pot.

The stew would be cooked over low heat for about three hours. The fava beans, having been cooked separately with spices, would be added at the end of the cooking time.

Some patés were made from the livers of fattened geese or duck; others were made out of olives, anchovies, garlic, and herbs. Lathered on bread, and consumed with wine, this was considered a meal.

Meat pies, consisting of pork sausage and wild herbs, complimented with the addition of mushrooms, garlic and parsley, were also enjoyed.

Living near the coast allowed for elaborate fish preparations using fresh fish (black bass, pike, rainbow trout, arctic char, eels, salmon, sea trout, monkfish), salted fish (usually cod) and shellfish (mussels, oysters and sea crickets, which were tiny crayfish-like creatures).

With "mountains, pastures, fertile soils, salt lagoons and the Mediterranean Sea at its disposal, not to mention a superb climate," [40] clearly there was a richness that existed in reference to gastronomy in the Languedoc area.

---

[40] http://www.frenchpropertylinks.com/essential/languedoc-food.html

Married to Jordan III, Seigneur de L'Isle-Jourdain, in 1175, Esclarmonde de Foix, a predestined name which meant *Light of the World* in Old Occitan language, had given birth to several children; namely, [1] Bernard, who would later inherit the County of Foix, [2] Guillamette, [3] Olive, [4] Othon de Terride, and [5] Bertrand, who would later become Baron de Launac.

It was amongst this household that Isabeau, born in 1195, had been raised since infancy.

The Cathars, knowing a great deal about herbalism, were successful healers and doctors. Isabeau knew that this was her destiny.

It had long been stipulated that she would foster with Beatriu de Blanchefort, the Cathari herbalist at Béziers, upon reaching the age of ten. There was also great pride in knowing that Beatriu was a relative of Bertrand de Blanchefort, the 6th Grand Master of the Knights Templar.

In the meantime, she had been apprenticing with Marquesia, an herbalist in L'Isle-Jourdain.

Esclarmonde was widowed in 1204, at the age of 49. Having been married for twenty-nine years, with "no regard for the material things of life, [she] left to her children the wealth and huge estates of their father." [41]

Her brother, Raymond Roger had been taken prisoner in 1203, so she returned home to Foix, with young Isabeau, now aged nine, to manage the Château in his absence.

---

[41]

http://www.rosicrucian.org/publications/digest/digest2_2011/04_web/09_hbernard/09_hbernard_112311.pdf

With the long flowing red-gold tresses and azure blue eyes of her forefathers, it is said that, when angered, Isabeau's eyes flashed sparks of black.

Marquesia was most impressed with the wealth of knowledge she had been able to share, in such a short time, with her young charge. In truth, it had been but two years since they had begun their apprenticing lessons.

Most meticulous in her studies, Isabeau was a delightful and intuitively guided child; she was able to remember, with ease and assuredness, everything that Marquesia had instructed; never, in the course of her years as an herbalist, had there been a more diligent student.

The ancient Egyptians, Greeks and Romans had utilized plants for medicinal uses. Many Greek and Roman writings on medicine, as on other subjects, had been preserved by the hand copying of manuscripts in monasteries.

As a result, it was the monasteries that had become the local centers of medical knowledge.

Folk medicine, however, revolved around the usage of herb gardens, with herbalists knowing that such herbs provided the raw materials for simple treatment of common disorders.

Isabeau knew that there were many ways to use herbs for healing.

She'd been taught that you could let the herb steep in hot or cold water; you could either reheat the concoction or drink it cool.

There were times, on the other hand, when roots, and heavy wooden plants, had to be simmered for the effects to be experienced.

When the herbs were too strong to ingest, a compress was made and applied to the infected area; a means through which the skin would allow for a smaller amount of the herb to be absorbed, slowly, by the body. You would soak a cotton cloth in the mixture, wringing out the excessive liquid, before applying to the affected area.

Extracts could be made, using oil, vinegar or alcohol, to treat ailments such as strained muscles, arthritis or inflammation.

A poultice could be made by suspending a sieve containing the fresh or dried herbs over boiling water, steaming them for a few minutes. After spreading the softened herbs onto a cloth, it would be applied to the affected area. This worked well for inflammation, bites and boils. You might also cover the compress with a bandage, leaving it for several hours at a time.

Salves were made by taking dried, or fresh, herbs, and covering then with water, wherein you would bring to the boil, simmering for about 30 minutes. After straining, you would add an equal amount of goose grease, simmering, once again, until the remaining water had evaporated. This is when you would add just enough beeswax to give the salve a thick consistency, immediately pouring the mixture into a jar, knowing that it would harden as it cooled.

Tinctures, similar to extracts, were made for individuals with weak digestion.

Upon taking a jar, the dried herbal mixture was placed on the bottom. After adding enough alcohol to cover the herbs, plus an additional inch, it would be left to sit for two weeks, before straining.

Eardrops were made by slicing garlic and then placing in a small amount of olive oil. After adding a few lavender flowers, you were required to leave it alone for several hours, before straining. As needed, you would warm small amounts of the eardrop oil by placing it over a cup of hot water, before adding to the ear and plugging with a cotton cloth.

In addition, Anise was used to combat flatulence; Betony was used to alleviate migraines; Chamomile was used to combat headaches; Cumin, while often used in poultices, was also used to combat flatulence; Mint was used for stomach problems; Nutmeg was used to aid digestion and relieve nausea; Rosemary was often positioned under a pillow to ward off nightmares, and Thyme was used to fumigate rooms against infection.

As well, placing an unpeeled onion in a dish, within the rooms of a home, would somehow absorb bacteria, as well as viruses, keeping the family healthy.

Cinnamon, one of the world's oldest healers, was used in the treatment of sinuses, colds, flu, indigestion and uterine problems.

Ginger was often used as an anti-inflammatory compound. As a carrier herb, meaning that ginger was an herb that would bind with other herbs, helping to "carry the other herbs deeper into the body's systems ... [increasing] their efficacy," [42] it was also known to "decrease blood pressure and heart rate [with] its circulatory stimulation properties ... [helping to] offset sluggish circulation." [43]

Cloves were used to both to freshen one's breath, an important part of one's oral hygiene, as well as to relieve toothache and acne.

---

[42] http://www.holisticbirds.com/pages/ginger0802.htm
[43] Ibid.

Fennel was often used to relieve lethargy and combat depression, while eating the leaves, stems and seeds, or making a leaf or seed tea, was known to contribute to weight loss. If chewed during fasting days, it was said to dull the appetite, as well as one's desire, for sweets.

While oregano oil was known to be a potent antiseptic, one that helped "to prevent infections as a result of burns," [44] oregano was also used to relax respiratory problems related to "asthma, bronchitis, cough, colds and flu, as well as inflammation of the mouth and throat." [45] Used to treat skin diseases and itching; so, too was it applied to stings and bites. [46]

In returning home to Foix, Esclarmonde now sought the expertise of València, the resident herbalist, knowing that Isabeau would remain under her care for one more year before making the trek to Béziers.

---

[44] http://www.livestrong.com/article/300782-burn-treatment-with-oregano-oil/
[45] http://www.bestantiagingsystems.com/1599/anti-aging-essential-oils/
[46] Ibid.

Chapter 10

When Roger, Count of Carcassonne, died in 1067 without issue, Béziers passed to his sister Ermengard, wife of Raymond-Bertrand Trencavel; the family of Isabeau's paternal grandmother.

Their lands "in the centre of the Languedoc gave the Trencavels considerable power in the 11th and 12th centuries. The Counts of Barcelona and Toulouse both had large territories to the east and west, and valued a potential alliance with a family that stood in the middle. For the most part, the Trencavels allied with the counts of Barcelona, who became the Kings of Aragon." [47]

Traveling from Foix to Béziers, took the better part of four days, averaging between 20 and 22 miles a day.

---

[47] http://www.midi-france.info/1914_trencavel.htm

Life in Béziers, for Isabeau, was very different from that which she'd been accustomed, the most significant being how close she was situated to the Mediterranean, making for warm to hot, dry summers and mild to cool, wet winters, albeit a slight change.

Located on a bluff above the River Orb, which flows into the Mediterranean Sea, Béziers owes its name to the Celts who ursurped the settlement long before the Romans arrived and rebuilt the city as a new colony (36 BC), situated on the original Herculean Way, later the Domitian Way, a Roman road that linked Italy with Iberia.

In fact, stones from the "Roman amphitheatre here were used to construct the city walls during the 3rd century. Béziers later became one of the seven cities of Septimania, along with Agde, Lodeve, Maguelonne, Nîmes, Toulouse and Uzès." [48]

Here in Béziers, it felt as if Isabeau was surrounded by a different culture, by a different history.

---

[48] http://www.languedoc-france.info/030109_beziers.htm

The Pont-Vieux, a stone bridge spanning the River Orb, was a site to behold unto itself; the majestic Cathédrale Saint Nazaire, on its hilltop perch, provided the most splendid views of the village and surrounding area. Both Église de Saint-Jacques, as built by Charlemagne, and Église de La Madeleine, dedicated to the Magdalene, were impressive structures as well.

Even the landscape was different.

While there were mountains nearby, albeit not like the mountains of home, the area was abundant in valleys and streams, forests and springs, caves and grottoes.

Beatriu de Blanchefort, the Cathari herbalist at Béziers, was simply delighted to have such a young and knowledgeable charge. Under her care, Isabeau became even more adept at identifying and locating medicinal herbs and plants.

It was not long before she, too, was regarded, most highly, as both healer as well as herbalist.

In fact, this was how she came to meet Jonathon Maquire.

Chapter 11

Isabeau was thirteen years old when Beatriu began allowing her to set off, sometimes for several days at a time, in search of the herbs, roots and seedlings that were needed for the apothecary at Béziers.

The area, abundant in valleys and streams, forests and springs, caves and grottoes, was one that she never grew tired of exploring, for this is where she felt closest to God(dess).

Privy to the gift of sight, there would be times, during many an exploration, when she would experience visions; images that, while they could be somewhat unnerving to the average layperson, she'd never yet understood.

On this particular spring day, she'd somehow found herself in a secluded glen, an area that had never before been visited or explored. In truth, she was quite delighted with herself. Always protected by her gift of intuitiveness, she was never afraid to be alone.

After a small meal of bread, cheese and wine, Isabeau decided to take a wee nap before investigating further. Immediately upon waking, she was quick to discover a young man, sitting a short distance away.

With hair as dark as her eyes would flash when she was angry, and the deepest emerald green eyes she had ever seen, framed by the darkest, curliest, lashes, so black that they look as if they had been blackened with soot, the very eyelashes she, herself, had always wanted, she thought him most handsome indeed; a fact that made her smile.

"Who might you be, kind sir?"

"You may call me ... Prince," was the reply.

"Hmmmm ... I know who you are ... Prince. You are one of the fae folk, sometimes called *le petit peuple*, *le bon peuple*, *le peuple des fées*, of the forest and meadows."

"How might you know this, mistress?"

"Long have I studied the arts of healing, magick and alchemy."

Prince smiled a slow and carefree smile. He inquired further with yet another question.

"What else do you know about me, about us?"

Isabeau had learned, long before, if one of the fae folk were to take a human to faerieland, they would never be able to return to the human world.

On the flip side, she had also learned if one of the fae folk were to take a human to a secluded glen, this would not be the case, for they would have the ability to return.

Secluded faerie glens are hidden by foliage and between rock walls, so they are generally hard to find, which is why she was still amazed at having discovered this spot on her own. Further intellectual reasoning told her that she had been intuitively guided to find this place.

Isabeau also knew that whilst in the confines of the glen, the human could eat of the food with no problem, whereas to eat of the food given by the fae in faerieland would forever trap the human in another dimension.

Prince, who was really Jonathan Maquire, known to family and friends simply as Jon, was surprisingly amazed at the knowledge of this young woman.

While he'd seen her many times before, on many a sojourn, feeling drawn to her in a way that could never be adequately described, in human terms, he'd never approached her before, until now.

With hair that blazed like golden fire, and eyes the deepest shade of azure blue, the color of the Mediterranean sea, Isabeau was a perfect match for his coal black locks and eyes of emerald green; together, they sported a most attractive looking pair.

"You are most resourceful in your knowledge, mistress."

Holding out his hand to her, this tall, radiant being, asked if she cared to join him in a stroll about his glen.

Although she was quite impressively tall for a young woman, standing 5 foot 10 inches, Isabeau found that she still had to tilt her head upwards to meet his gaze.

"I never knew that one could claim ownership of such beauty as created by God(dess)," was her quick reply, before placing her hand in his.

Prince simply answered with an ethereal smile that hinted at secrets, ages old.

They spent the entirety of their day together; strolling and talking, getting to know one another whilst resting in the shelter of the massive evergreen Holly Oak trees.

The oak, a most sacred and holy tree to the fae, is considered the tree of endurance and triumph. In keeping, the oak leaf is referred to as the giver of life, meaning that it is the holder of the essence of the tree, bringing luck, health and protection to those who believed in its power. [49]

Associated with unicorns, and revered by the Druids, there were special spirits that dwelled within these Holly trees.

---

[49] http://www.celticattic.com/olde_world/myths/oak_lore.htm

It had long been said that it is the "Holly Man in the tree that bears prickly Holly, and the Holly Woman within that gives forth smooth and variegated leaves." [50]

Isabeau was learning that the leaf of the Holly Oak could be dried and incorporated into a tea for the treatment of fevers, bladder problems and bronchitis; likewise, the juice of the fresh leaf was helpful in the treatment of yellowed skin. While you were not to eat of the berries, because they were poisonous, hanging a sprig of Holly in the home was said to ensure protection as well as good luck.

Whilst Prince was not his true name, Isabeau had learned that he was indeed a *real* Prince of the faerie realm; a human-sized, unbelievably beautiful being, he was a Sidhe, called forth to help a deserving human, but only visible in the presence of a human.

He'd further disclosed that he was also the guardian of this glen.

---

[50] http://dutchie.org/holly-lore/

Isabeau told him about the circumstances surrounding her birth; that she was the healer, long awaited by the Cathari. She'd further disclosed that she had the gift of sight, able to see the fae folk of the forest and meadows.

Although not yet experienced, Prince told her that she also had the gift of second sight.

Isabeau further shared what she knew; namely, that roses attracted the faerie people and that a four leaf clover could always be used to break a faerie spell.

"Not only are you marvelously resourceful in your knowledge, mistress, as well you know, but you are as beautiful as a faerie."

Looking deep into his eyes, Isabeau was quick to acknowledge the compliment with an ethereal smile of her own.

Chapter 12

Isabeau quickly developed a unique relationship with one Jonathon (Jon) Maguire, and yes, he did eventually disclose his name, not caring one whit if the giving of his name meant that she now had power over him; completely entranced, he knew that he had found his soul mate.

The Sidhe (pronounced shee) are often described as "a race of majestic appearance and marvelous beauty, in form human, yet in nature divine." [51]

With "distinct tribes, ruled over by fairy kings and queens in each territory," [52] they are also referred to "as the *gentry* on account of their tall, noble appearance and silvery sweet speech." [53]

---

[51]

http://www.bibliotecapleyades.net/merovingians/blueapples/blueapples_05.htm

[52] http://celticsociety.freeservers.com/sidhe.html

[53] Ibid.

The glen, itself, was a very powerful vortex area whereby one could gain access to the innerworld home of the Tuatha Dé Danann (pronounced thoo-AH-huh duh-DAH-nun), a people of superior intelligence and artistic skill who, having fought wars in the past, were now opposed to the same.

Descended from the Túatha Dé Danann, Jonathan was a Túath Druid with special powers, for not only did he possess the gift of knowledge, but, so, too, would a drink, given from his hands, heal any wound, or cure any disease.

The Túatha Dé Danann were known to be "the finest smiths, jewellers, poets and musicians of their time; they were the Lords of fearless warriors and gifted horsemen; they were a righteous, meticulous people who maintained standards of conduct in areas of their social life where such standards were considered essential for the harmonious order of society." [54]

---

[54]

http://www.bibliotecapleyades.net/ciencia/ciencia_tuathadedanaan01.htm

Considerable importance was laid "upon honesty and truth in one's words and one's dealings; the maintenance and conservation of the natural environment was paramount. Emphasis was also laid on hospitality and courtly behavior to one's peers or guests, the honoring of one's ancestors and heroes, and the maintenance of extended family ties through fostering." [55]

Theirs was a race "centered on their spirituality, which itself was centered on gnosis and transcendent consciousness." [56]

Generally benign until angered by some foolish action of a human, the Sidhe, down through the ages, "have been in contact with mortals giving protection, healing and even teaching some of their skills to mortals." [57]

The word Sidhe can also mean profound peace, in that "spiritual vibrancy comes from being in harmony with, and

---

[55]

http://www.bibliotecapleyades.net/ciencia/ciencia_tuathadedanaan01.htm
[56] Ibid.
[57] http://www.shee-eire.com/Magic&Mythology/Fairylore/Sidhe/page%201.htm

accepting, one's own nature; being in harmony with one's tribe, family or wider community; from being in harmony with one's ancestral line and their expectations (recalling the link between the burial mounds and the creatures dwelling within them); from being in harmony with one's Gods and the forces of the cosmos. Peace here does not mean just sitting quietly, but a deep sense of balance, harmony, belonging, and attunement," [58] which, as guardian of the glen, was *exactly* how Jonathan felt.

Living in the Otherworld, often referred to as faerieland, he was able to journey into the human world via the portal of the glen.

Whatever the "jargon and conceptualisation, the basic idea is of a world that runs alongside, and often overlaps with," [59] that of the human world.

---

[58] http://druidnetwork.org/learning/courses/online/polytheist/five
[59] Ibid.

"You, my dearest Isabeau, are as wise as the Túatha Dé Danann."

"Do tell me more," she acknowledged with a coquettish smile.

"Firstly, you are able to connect with nature, whilst also acknowledging how beautiful and powerful she is. All can learn from Mother Nature, the very best teacher of balance, if they were so inclined. So, too, does she enable you to see, when properly attuned, as are you, the fluctuation that also exists within the balance of life, death and re-birth."

Jon toyed with a single blade of grass before continuing, almost daydreaming, instead, that it were a silken strand of burnished gold.

"Secondly, you are so very connected with spirit, always remembering to be thankful when you are in a spiritual place, such as the faerie forest and this glen.

"In reference to the herbs that you avail of, it is through your hands that love and healing spring forth. You feel good about the service that you are able to provide. Lastly, you demonstrate considerable responsibility and foresight, making decisions with serious thought.

"In truth, dearest Isabeau, you are able to see the results from integrating all of these intertwined components. You both recognize and acknowledge that examining decisions with your heart, body and mind is the essential conjoining; an action that allows you to continue to discover the ebb and flow of life. Each time you make use of your newly discovered wisdom, you make much better choices for everyone involved, yourself included.

"A seeker of truth, you also strive for kinship with Nature and your fellow beings. Most importantly, so, too, do you have the wisdom to allow others to reap their consequences for themselves, knowing this to be the most loving thing you can do for them, thereby granting them the opportunity to experience their own instruction, be it enlightened or otherwise; hence, my initial comment being that you are as wise as the Túatha Dé Danann, my people."

"Thank you for this commendation, milord. In truth, I am hoping that you might be able to share more with me about your Druid ancestry; I am most keen to learn more."

"Most certainly, milady," Jon quickly replied.

"There are three Druidic mysteries that have existed since time immemorial.

"The Ancients believed "that the Cosmos comes into being according to the inner living and growing pattern that is the inspiration of creative genius. It is this pattern, and the process that creates it, that we call the Art. From the primordial chaos of potential, the Art brings forth the majesty of the Cosmos, growing and weaving like the living branches of the World Tree. The Art lives within each thing, as it does in the Cosmos entire; to honor the Art is to honor the sacred beauty that is the One and the All." [60] This, the first of the mysteries, is a belief, as well as an understanding, that you also aspire to.

---

[60] http://tuathadebrighid.net/html/tuatha_de_brighid_druidry_-_th.html

"The Druids of Old, of which I am but one in a long familial line, taught "that it is by its Truth that each thing grows into fullness. It is Truth that is the seed, the root, and the flowering of virtue; so, too, is it Truth that is the ultimate essence of the Art. It is by Truth that all good things come to be, and it is by Truth that all good things flourish. It is by Truth that honorable power is gained and used, in beauty, in healing, and in magic. To honor Truth is to honor the sacred meaning and purpose of each life." [61] This second mystery speaks to how you compose yourself as both herbalist as well as healer.

"The third mystery states that as "blood and bone and spirit, we spring from the same Source as the greatest of stars and smallest of atoms. Nothing exists apart from this Kinship, and the ties of Kinship, in all its guises, are Holy. All human beings exist as part of a family, a Whole, and it is by how they treat the ties, the relationships, and the mutual obligations inherent in being a part, as well as a whole, that they fulfill their Truth and their Art. To honor Kinship is to

---

[61] http://tuathadebrighid.net/html/tuatha_de_brighid_druidry_-_th.html

honor the sacred ties, and the giving, and the taking, within the living Cosmos." [62] You full well understand, and live, this third mystery.

"Perhaps, then, based on your shared words, I am a Druidess of sorts."

Jonathan smiled, a most knowing smile, before answering.

"As Druids, "we live and grow though and with the Universe. It is our task to allow the Light that dwells at the core of all things to illumine our lives, and times, and places, and reveal them for the sacred things that they are." [63] So, yes, in answer to your question, my dearest Isabeau, I see you as a Druidess of the highest order."

---

[62] http://tuathadebrighid.net/html/tuatha_de_brighid_druidry_-th1.html

[63] Ibid.

Chapter 13

In the Languedoc, political control "was divided among many local lords and town councils. There was little fighting in the area and a fairly sophisticated polity. Western Mediterranean France, itself, was, at that time, divided between the Crown of Aragon and the county of Toulouse." [64]

With the Cathar movement growing to represent a popular mass movement, the faith attracted many followers and sympathizers.

The Roman Catholic Church, alarmed by the spread of dualistic Cathar teachings, "perceived the movement as a well-organiscd opponent on a scale that had not been seen since the days of Arianism and Marcionism." [65]

---

[64] http://en.wikipedia.org/wiki/Albigensian_Crusade
[65] Ibid.

Becoming Pope in 1198, Innocent III resolved to deal with the Cathars, but attempts at peaceful conversion had met with little success.

The Cathar leadership "was protected by powerful nobles, and some bishops, allegedly resentful of papal authority in their sees, were not hostile toward the belief. In 1204, the Pope suspended the authority of some of those bishops and appointed papal legates to act in his name. In 1206, he sought support for wider action against the Cathars from the nobles of the Languedoc," [66] excommunicating those who supported Catharism.

Raymond VI, Count of Toulouse, close relative to Raymond Roger, refused to assist; he was excommunicated in May 1207.

The Pope then "called upon the French king, Philippe II, to act against those nobles who permitted Catharism, but Philippe declined to act. Count Raymond met with the papal legate, Pierre de Castelnau, in January 1208, and after an

---

[66] http://en.wikipedia.org/wiki/Albigensian_Crusade

angry meeting, Castelnau was murdered the following day. The Pope reacted to the murder by issuing a bull declaring a crusade against Languedoc, offering the land of the heretics to any who would fight." [67]

It was this offer of land that drew the northern French nobility into conflict with the nobles of the south.

---

[67] http://en.wikipedia.org/wiki/Albigensian_Crusade

Chapter 14

Location: Château de Béziers, Languedoc, southern France

Time: July 20, 1209

At dawn, Isabeau set off for the glen. She had packed enough to sustain her for four or five days, her longest trek yet, whilst also collecting herbs, roots and seedlings for Beatriu de Blanchefort.

Unbeknownst to Isabeau, there was a complete and utter darkness fast approaching.

Chapter 15

Location: Château de Béziers, Languedoc, southern France
Time: July 22, 1209, the feast day of St. Mary Magdalene

Béziers, a city in Southern France, near the Mediterranean, and across from Italy, was home to Cathars, a peaceable people, also known as Albigenses, because of their association with the city of Albi.

Raymond Roger of Trencavel was Viscount of Béziers and Albi (making him a vassal of the Count of Toulouse); so, too, was he Viscount of Carcassonne and the Razès (making him a vassal of the Count of Barcelona).

With Béziers being his second seat of power, he, himself, lived in the Château Comtal (built by his ancestors in the 11th century) as located in the fortified hill town of Carcassonne.

In a time when the Roman Catholic Church was already rich and corrupt, the faith of the Cathars was attracting many followers.

As a result, the Pope offered "men pardon for their sins if they would undertake a crusade against the heretics," [68] with the prospect of loot, as well as land, exciting many to join the army, given this southern area of considerable affluence.

In total, there were about 200 Cathars residing in Béziers, amidst a much greater population of sympathetic Catholics.

It was on this day that a "group of defenders rode out with white pennants shooting arrows at the Crusaders, killing one. Furious, a bunch of rag-tag camp followers, without proper weapons, rushed the walls. Beziers had not expected an attack so soon; the walls were not properly manned. Defenders fled. Within three hours, the Crusaders had taken a city that they had thought they would have to beseige for several months." [69]

As the crusading army sacked and looted Béziers, most indiscriminately, the townspeople retreated to the sanctuary of the churches.

---

[68] http://www.christianity.com/ChurchHistory/11629815/
[69] Ibid.

When asked how to discern Cathar from Catholic, it was the Cistercian abbot-commander, Arnaud Amaury, who replied: *Caedite eos ... Novit enim Dominus qui sunt eius ...* meaning *Kill them all. God will recognize his own.*

Many of the Catholic citizens sought refuge in the Church dedicated to Mary Magdalene. While this Church was set alight, the rest of the town was put to the sword.

Could it be that the fall of Béziers had doomed the Cathars?

Chapter 16

It was on Isabeau's fourteenth birthday, July 22, 1209, that all of the residents of Béziers were massacred. So, too, was the Roman-Gothic church of La Madeleine a scene of great bloodshed.

There were 20,000 that perished that fateful day, regardless of rank, age or sex, all save Isabeau.

A noble member of the Cathari population, albeit of illegitimate birth, Jon vowed to keep her safe and free from harm.

In keeping with her truthfulness, kindness, spiritual vibrancy, kinship with Nature, foresight and applied wisdom to the totality of all life, Isabeau was accorded a special dispensation from King Tuathal and Queen Maeve, Jon's parents; a dispensation that allowed her to both live in faerieland, and return to the human world, alongside Jon.

As a result, Isabeau was able to work closely with the fae folk over the course of the next thirty years.

Gleaning from their knowledge, and always according them the utmost privacy, she came to be revered amongst the Túatha Dé Danann; almost akin to the maintaining of extended family ties through fostering.

Chapter 17

At age forty-four, Isabeau did not look a day older than twenty-four. Under the guidance and protection of the fae folk, she had hardly aged at all. *Some people age well, whilst others do not* was always her reply.

Knowing that she could not, in all honesty, remain with the fae forever, she had continued to consult with Jon as to the time when she could return to live amongst her own people.

"My dearest Jon, as much as I hate to leave you, and the life we have created, I am obliged to return to my people. It is my wish to return to my youthful days at the Château of my father in Foix. In truth, I hope to see my brother, Roger Bernard, so that we may speak of my deceased father."

Acknowledging her words with a sad smile, Jon assured her that he would let her know when it was safe to return.

Several weeks later, an elated Isabeau was able to begin her most cautious return to Foix.

As a young girl of ten, she remembered the trip from Foix to Béziers taking the better part of four days, averaging between 20 and 22 miles a day. Retracing her steps without a horse, the trip was going to take considerably longer, but she knew how to easily keep to the hidden trails.

Chapter 18

A little over one month later, Isabeau arrived at Foix. Her elation, however, quickly changed to one of despondency.

Roger Bernard refused to see her, stating that his sister *had died at Béziers some thirty years prior.* The aged townsfolk clearly believed that black magick was afoot.

The only choice she had was to journey slightly farther north, to Muret, near Toulouse, to meet up with her sister Cécile, wife of Bernard V, Count of Comminges. After refreshing her supplies, she began traveling anew.

On the outskirts of Muret, however, something unexpected and shocking happened; she was quickly intercepted by several members of the Dominican Order.

Could it be that she had been turned in by her own brother?

Had he known where she would attempt to go?

With Dominic having established a religious community in Toulouse in 1214, Pope Gregory IX "assigned the duty of carrying out inquisitions to [his] Dominican Order." [70] [71]

Making use of inquisitorial procedures, they "judged heresy alone, using the local authorities to establish a tribunal and to prosecute heretics," [72] with a Grand Inquisitor heading each Inquisition; the purpose being to discover, and eliminate any vestiges of Cathar belief left after the Albigensian Crusades.

Before the Crusades, the Languedoc, under the Counts of Toulouse, had been "the most civilized land in Europe. People here had preferred simple asceticism to venality and corruption. Learning had been highly valued. Literacy had been widespread, and popular literature had developed earlier than anywhere else in Europe. Religious tolerance had been widely practiced. The Languedoc had been the home of courtly love, poetry, romance, chivalry and the

---

[70] http://en.wikipedia.org/wiki/Dominican_Order
[71] http://en.wikipedia.org/wiki/Inquisition
[72] Ibid.

troubadours. All this was swept away by the Albigensian Crusade and the Inquisition." [73]

Initially made welcome "by the Catholic community, the Inquisition soon came to be widely hated throughout the Languedoc by Jews, Cathars, Waldensians and Catholics alike, including local priests and bishops. Part of the reason was that the Inquisition, with its papal backing, was able to ignore the established power structure. It acted independently of, and often against, the interests of local potentates, bishops, lords and municipal councils alike." [74]

Unsurprisingly, the Inquisitors were often "attacked when they appeared in public without their armed guards," [75] while their practice "of digging up the bodies of supposed heretics in cemeteries, excited particular local ire." [76]

Following the investigation and trial, possible punishments included "wearing a yellow cross for life, banishment,

_____

[73] http://www.cathar.info/1209_inquisition.htm
[74] Ibid.
[75] Ibid.
[76] Ibid.

public recantation, or, occasionally, long-term imprisonment," [77] thereby opening those convicted up to "the possibility of various corporal punishments, including being burned at the stake." [78]

Execution was "neither performed by the Church, nor was it a sentence available to the officials involved in the inquisition, who, as clerics, were forbidden to kill." [79]

However, they generally "preferred not to hand over heretics to the secular arm for execution, if they could persuade the heretic to repent: *Ecclesia non novit sanguine* [for] execution was to admit defeat, that the Church was unable to save a soul from heresy, which was the goal of the inquisition." [80]

Housed in a dark, dank, cell, until ready to be tried by the Inquisition, Isabeau was quick to catch the chill that led to her death.

---

[77] http://en.wikipedia.org/wiki/Medieval_Inquisition
[78] Ibid.
[79] Ibid.
[80] Ibid.

Completely distraught, at having misread the signs, Jon vowed to return, at some point, in the future, whereby he would be able to keep her safe, but this time as a human, forsaking his noble and immortal birthright.

Chapter 19

Location: Fay O'Shea Fine Arts

With pictures and memories so vivid, painting them came both easily and naturally to Michaela.

Fay O'Shea Fine Arts, the world renowned gallery where her paintings were featured, on a regular basis, was situated in Flagstaff, Arizona.

Being Irish, Michaela's favorite holiday, quite naturally, was St. Patrick's Day.

March 17, 2009, found her standing in front of her favorite painting; one of Jon, with the most amazingly deep emerald green eyes, framed by the darkest, curliest, lashes, so black that they look as if they had been blackened with soot.

Sipping on a hot mug of Green and Fruity Rooibos, [81] similar to that of green tea, but with a smooth, fresh taste,

---

[81] http://www.davidstea.com/our-teas/rooibos/green-and-fruity

topped up with the tropical flavors of papaya, apple, mango and peach, a drink most fitting for the day in question, an unknown male came to stand beside her, commenting on the aliveness that the painting exuded, almost as if it had been an actual photograph.

Smiling to herself, albeit sadly, and mumbling a few words in agreement, Michaela continued to remain transfixed by the painting; existing in her own little trance, a cocoon, of sorts, that no one else had ever been able to enter.

"Why are you so drawn to the painting?" he queried.

"It is someone that I once knew very well," she responded.

"He appears to have a medieval air about him."

"You are very discerning. In truth, I met him when I was fourteen, back in 1209, some eight hundred years ago," was the honest reply.

"Ah, yes, *time will tell, my wee one*," was the immediate response.

Hearing the very phrase that Jon had always used, when they would speak of their shared dreams, Michaela's hands began to shake.

Reaching out to take the mug, that was, then, placed on a nearby table, the unknown male quickly returned to stand in front of her.

A few inches shy of six feet, Michaela had to tilt her head up to get a solid look at the gentleman who had been attempting to converse with her, for her eyes were now directly centered with his chest.

Taking a deep breath, she slowly raised her face. To her complete, and utter, astonishment, she found herself looking into the all-too familiar, most amazingly deep emerald green eyes, framed by the darkest, curlicst, lashcs, so black that they look as if they had been blackened with soot.

Jon smiled the most magnificent of smiles, opening his arms wide. Enveloped in their warmth, Michaela cried tears of utter joy and relief, for they had both come home; this time, for good.

[1] Aznar of Comminges and Couserans.

[2] Roger I of Carcassonne, also known as Roger II of Comminges the Elder, was the Count of Carcassonne, Couserans and Comminges.

[3] Bernard-Roger, founder of the House of Foix. It was during his father's lifetime that he married Arsinde, or Garsenda, the heiress of the county of Bigorre.

[4] Roger I of Foix, became the first Count of Foix, which included the castles of Castelpenet, Roquemaure, Lordat, and several within the county of Toulouse. He never married.

[5] Pierre-Bernard, brother of Roger I, inherited the title of Count of Foix. He married Ledgarde.

[6] Roger II, Count of Foix, married Estefania of Besalú (second wife).

[7] Roger III, Count of Foix, married Jimena of Barcelona (second wife).

[8] Roger-Bernard I, Count of Foix, married Cécile Trencavel of Béziers.

→ Raymond Roger (born circa 1152), Count of Foix, married Philippa of Montcada.

→ Esclarmonde de Foix (born circa 1155) married Jordan III, Seigneur de L'Isle-Jourdain.

SOURCES

http://genealogiequebec.info/testphp/info.php?no=172960

http://genealogiequebec.info/testphp/info.php?no=174719

http://en.wikipedia.org/wiki/Roger_I_of_Carcassonne

http://en.wikipedia.org/wiki/Bernard-
Roger,_Count_of_Bigorre

http://en.wikipedia.org/wiki/Count_of_Foix

http://en.wikipedia.org/wiki/Raimond-Roger_of_Foix

http://en.wikipedia.org/wiki/Esclarmonde_of_Foix

http://en.wikipedia.org/wiki/Counts_of_comminges

http://fmg.ac/Projects/MedLands/GASCONY.htm#_Toc274 803890

http://en.wikipedia.org/wiki/Dukes_of_Gascony

http://en.wikipedia.org/wiki/Aznar_Gal%C3%ADndez_I

http://en.wikipedia.org/wiki/Galindo_Azn%C3%A1rez_I

http://en.wikipedia.org/wiki/Aznar_Gal%C3%ADndez_II

http://genealogy.euweb.cz/foix/foix1.html#RB1

http://genealogy.euweb.cz/foix/foix2.html

http://genealogy.euweb.cz/foix/foix1.html#CRT

http://genealogy.euweb.cz/barcelona/barcelona1.html#EG2

http://fr.wikipedia.org/wiki/Liste_des_comtes_de_Comming es

Having lived a full life, as both wife and mother, it was not long thereafter before Esclarmonde was able to turn her complete and undivided attention to the Cathar church, devoting herself to the life she had long yearned for.

Receiving the Cathar sacrament, the consolamentum, at the hands of the Cathar bishop, Guilabert de Castres, in 1206 in Fanjeaux, Esclarmonde was now both Parfaite as well as Archdeaconness; the ceremony was conducted in the presence of her brother, Raymond Roger de Foix. [82][83][84]

The consolamentum "was a form of initiation by the laying on of hands thought to go back all the way to the time of Christ and the apostles." [85] Thereafter, she took up

---

[82]

http://www.rosicrucian.org/publications/digest/digest2_2011/04_web/09_hbernard/09_hbernard_112311.pdf

[83] http://en.wikipedia.org/wiki/Esclarmonde_of_Foix

[84] http://www.cathar.info/120516_esclarmonde.htm

[85]

http://www.dhaxem.com/data/handt/The_Great_Esclarmonde_of_the_Cathars.pdf

residence in Pamiers. [86] It is thought that she was responsible for advising Raymond de Pereilha to refortify the Castle at Montségur in preparation for the likely assaults by the French Catholic Crusaders. [87]

In 1207, Esclarmonde took part in, and quite probably organised, the Colloquy of Pamiers (also called the Colloquy of Montréal), the last public debate between the Cathars and the Roman Catholic Church whose representatives were led by Dominic de Guzmán (later Saint Dominic). [88]

It was at this very debate, in fact, that Esclarmonde tried to speak, "only to be admonished by a representative of the Roman Church [who uttered the following words]: *go to your spinning madam. It is not proper for you to speak in a debate of this sort.* [89]

---

[86]

http://www.dhaxem.com/data/handt/The_Great_Esclarmonde_of_the_Cathars.pdf

[87] Ibid.

[88] Ibid.

[89] Ibid.

This was a substantial faux pas, one quite obvious to an educated Occitan audience, and yet, to this day, "the Church seems to have not understood what Catharism was/is about and why their representatives lost in these debates so comprehensively, or so consistently." [90]

Esclarmonde and her sister-in-law, Philippa Montcada, jointly "ran a House for Parfaites at Dun in the Pyrénées. A sort of prototype convent, it functioned as a school for the education of girls and as a sort of retirement home for aged Parfaites. Esclarmonde is credited with opening a number of hospitals, schools and Cathar convents, something the Roman Church had not done previously, but started to do later as part of its concerted effort to win credibility as an organization of faith." [91]

Esclarmonde is believed to have died in 1215.

---

[90]

http://www.dhaxem.com/data/handt/The_Great_Esclarmonde_of_the_Cathars.pdf

[91] Ibid.

The fact "that she has no grave is hardly surprising considering the lengths to which the heretics were forced to go to hide the bodies of their loved ones from the crusaders who, believing in physical resurrection at the end of time, were prone to dismembering, or otherwise violating the remains of those who escaped them in life." [92]

---

[92]

http://www.dhaxem.com/data/handt/The_Great_Esclarmonde_of_the_Cathars.pdf

The Cathars were not only aware of the laws of spirituality, but they also had extensive medical knowledge. Progress of their medicine followed in the footsteps of Hippocrates, with a scientific study and analysis of the body and all of its needs.

The Cathars realised that the state of the body reflects the thoughts and the deeds of a person.

The Cathar perfecti (or parfaits), who were also healers, travelled amongst the people and above all, taught the laws by which to live a pure lifestyle that would be conducive to health.

The Cathars were aware of the importance of food, and also, that a pure Soul would long only for pure, natural nutrition, obtained without the suffering to warm-blooded animals.

© http://www.dhaxem.com/the_cathars.htm

Reprinted herein with permission (from Corascendea)

The <u>first and most important law</u> of the Universe is that positive energy is stronger than negative energy.

The core of every soul is positive.

A turn took place when consciousness became able to construct concepts which were not directly related to the existence of the physical forms carrying it.

The forms started thinking, and after realizing the existence of individuality, they progressed to comparison, projection, and desire. The ego was born. With it came temptation.

Unconscious of the existence of the laws of the Universe, the life forms became receptacles of negativity. Jealousy, greed, and hate entered the consciousness and a long journey of suffering had started.

Souls resisting temptation, better than others, were becoming stronger. They were attracting more positive energy, whereas Souls giving in to negativity remained small and depleted.

They compensated by seeking the proximity of other like Souls, and by polarizing against the stronger Souls.

Like attracts like, is the <u>second law</u> of the Universe.

Another breakthrough took place after some Souls recognized the pattern of cause and effect directly connected to their own actions.

Negative actions resulted in their own suffering.

The process of learning had started, leading to the formation of Soul groups with different levels of knowledge and ability.

Increased consciousness leads to increased power, is <u>the third law</u> of the Universe.

Acquisition of all knowledge by a part of the consciousness leads to an accelerated growth of the whole of the consciousness is <u>the fourth law</u> of the Universe.

When all consciousnesses acquire all existing knowledge and when they completely purify, then all Souls will be one, and one with God.

For as long as there is incomplete consciousness, there is a need for evolution, is the fifth law of the Universe.

The stage when God will be all there is, in chronological terms, is many millions of years ahead. Before it happens, each and every consciousness will have to undergo purification.

Resistance makes suffering and pain worse.

The final battle between Good and Evil will consist of purification of ill will by suffering. Extreme pain renders ill will harmless, converting it back to objective energy.

Negative energy can be made neutral only by exposure to negative energy, is the sixth law of the Universe.

Any negative energy which becomes released will return to its original objective form in which it will not represent a threat to anyone. After that, there will be no more suffering and love will prevail.

The seventh law of the Universe is that negative energies are harmful only if they are a part of a consciousness.

A soul is a consciousness consisting of a specific configuration of wisdom accumulated through experiences.

There is a complete continuity of the Soul between its lifetimes and the stages out of the body.

During the brief periods of incarnation, the Soul tests its wisdom and gains new experiences, just as school children would test their knowledge of physics in an experimental laboratory.

More complex lessons span more than one lifetime, whilst unfolding in different sets of circumstances, the purpose of which it is to re-affirm relevant understanding within the Soul from as many angles as possible.

A Soul grows with every accomplished piece of an understanding.

A purified complete Soul need not incarnate further.

Because the path that leads to completeness is very demanding, few Souls choose it.

The majority of Souls settle for the more comfortable and easier option of their own incompleteness, whilst specializing in some area of competence which naturally suits them. Once reaching an appropriate level of training, and after completing purification, such Souls, too, need not incarnate further.

Their final roles can, on the whole, be described as ancillary, whereas the roles of Souls that reach their own completeness can be described as creative and managerial.

Creation on the Soul plane, energy is all there is.

Because a Soul turns its ideas into energy, a Soul capable of creating knowledge, in effect, creates a new reality for itself and others.

Hence the subjective God, the perfect Soul, is also the Creator.

As the gradual surrender of the ego takes place as part of a Soul's learning process, the Soul becomes increasingly capable of feeling emotions that are not directly connected to its own survival or well-being.

A Divine Soul, having completely surrendered its ego, is capable of loving others most.

If looking at the One, comparably to the Sun, rays of love can be seen radiating from within its Divine centre towards the periphery.

As the rays of the Divine love pass through the layers, they are absorbed and gradually replaced with the love of the inhabitants of those layers, who radiate their love further down towards the periphery.

Each Soul gets what it has earned, and love is earned by loving others.

© http://www.dhaxem.com/documents/

CATHAR_TESTAMENT.pdf

Reprinted herein with permission (from Corascendea)

A living being, capable of developing individual relationships and of bonding with others, is a Soul in a body, not a body with a Soul. The body is a possession that expires.

The body is lent to a Soul for the duration of a lifetime. Not just water, but all elements that make up and aid life, are in constant circulation; these are used as tools for shaping experiences through which Souls grow and purify.

To develop one's spiritual awareness means to develop the ability to think beyond the matter, to realize what the essence of human existence is, and what that potential may be.

If a Soul, incarnated in a human body, chooses to behave differently than that which is expected from humans, its future existence will reflect its desires and actions.

No Soul has an unconditional right to existence as a specific consciousness.

A Soul is a configuration of particles of energy. In cases of an extreme violation, against behaviour appropriate to the incarnation, the particles making up the Soul are returned into circulation, similarly to the remains of a physical body.

History has noted shifts in the presence, or in the volume, of life-forms. The disappearance of certain species whilst others remain, and/or their numbers increase, is not solely a matter of ecological changes.

The existing species and their proportions also fit the need for suitable forms of incarnation. Everything in the Universe makes sense at the Divine level.

Spirituality is such a used, abused, and often misunderstood term; one that can only be understood through learning about oneself and the accumulation of realizations.

In addition, it also requires the willingness to acknowledge the constructive content behind all experiences and their outcomes, beyond even their own subjective views, including the views of other people.

True spirituality does not require faith, making it incompatible with dogma.

While spirituality liberates the mind, teaches self-respect, and encourages us to take responsibility for our own actions, dogma makes the person feel small, dependent, and susceptible to the submitting of their own will, and, sometimes, even their own conscience, to status and power.

Dogma builds on the division between humans and God.

True spirituality brings the person closer to God.

Continuing to promote a division between man and God is both a sign of clandestine atheism as well as a desire to halt progress with a selective view to maintaining, or gaining, power, or influence, over others.

The only path to wealth is through the acquisition of realisations.

Enlightenment leads to the recognition that matter is worthless, and that it merely serves to represent alienation.

Any group, or organisation claiming to be one of faith, while accumulating political power and material wealth, is false.

They aim to exploit the desire of others, in their desire to find the path to God, for their own worldly gains.

True spirituality liberates one from fear.

A person on a conscious path to God would not fear undeserved harm, because harm only comes from one's own inappropriate and impure thoughts and actions; it becomes their aim in life, then, to purify such.

Only an un-awakened Soul would conceive the desire to interfere with the Divine course of events.

Abuse of others does not represent power. It is a sign of ignorance. Conscious abuse of others is a form of self-destruction.

Those on the genuine spiritual path are seeking to become a harmoniously creative part of the process.

Self-improvement and growth are the only way to fulfilment and eternal bliss.

The Essence of Healing

People tend to imagine that healing means the mending of physical defects and imbalances; this is *not* the correct perception of the term.

From the spiritual point of view, a physical or mental condition may be helpful to one in their fulfilling the purpose of life, which means, that it is the illness which heals the person and their Soul. The body, then, is granted a reprieve only after the Soul has learned from, or been purified through, the illness.

In its truest form, healing means maturing into the lessons that have been specifically facilitated by the experience.

Some people have genuinely thought that by becoming a healer (as in Reiki) that they could help themselves and others out of difficulty; such expectations are destined to be short lived. Any spiritual endeavours can only speed up the processes which are inevitable, and which, therefore, propel the Soul into the next stage; they cannot change them.

The level to which people consciously, or unconsciously, adhere to the Divine Laws, which govern all aspects of life, affects the degree to which they can heal.

Only a fully enlightened person will be free of all disease. With age, the body increasingly becomes the outer reflection of the person inside.

Spirituality and healing carry the same content, meaning that only people prepared to undertake additional challenges should seek a more intense spiritual path.

Catharism is the True Christianity

Between 1242 and 1244, Bertrand Marty, the spiritual leader of the Cathars, managed to share, at Montségur, with three hundred and thirty of the most enlightened perfects, his full realisation of the Divine Order, along with the correct interpretation of the incarnation of Christ, and of Jesus Christ being the Son of God, the Father.

The interpretation of the Church has been twisted.

The Church cannot define God, nor, it admits, can it explain the essence of the Trinity.

The Church, however, does not appear as equally uncertain about its own assets and deposits.

The Cathars were a genuine group of Christians, living what they preached; hence, the appeal of the Cathar lifestyle to the larger Catholic communities was huge.

When the spread of Catharism threatened the wealth and the political power of the Church, it was then that Rome initiated their plan for complete genocide.

The Inquisition was established with the aim to quash any traces of a revival. Over subsequent centuries, the Church only tolerated those who submitted to its worldly power.

In today's world, it takes pages to describe a single word that meant honour to Cathars. In Occitan, the language of the Languedoc, that word was Paratge. [93]

---

[93] http://www.dhaxem.com/data/handt/Cathar_Honour.pdf

Whole nations can be annihilated, but Truth cannot be destroyed.

For hundreds of years, brave individuals and groups have secretly kept the Cathar message alive.

Rewritten in modern language in 2006, the Divine Order of the Cathar Testament stands tall as the only comprehensive doctrine that appropriately describes the relationship between God and man.

© http://www.dhaxem.com/spiritual1.htm

Reprinted herein with permission (from Corascendea)

In reference to cancer, science has tried, and failed, to find a cure, while miraculous disappearances continue to prove that one exists.

Stress and trauma are *not* the cause of cancer.

If you, or a loved one, were diagnosed, the most important thing you need to know is that *cancer is on your side*.

If you deal with it to the best of your ability, you will make progress.

If you hide yourself in a sweet scented incense cloud, this could result in the missing of a revealing journey. Likewise, you would not be taking charge; which means that the cancer would have to do your work for you.

In choosing to hurl bricks, mindlessly, at the cancer, you both lose.

You alone have the choice.

No one can heal another person's cancer. The individual with the cancer is the only one who can heal him (her) self.

The Dhaxem Approach to Cancer

Cancer is not a tragedy, and neither is it a curse; it is an experience.

Cancer starts in the Soul, prior to incarnation, and its purpose is to heal the Soul. Embracing the experience, and taking a positive stance, is the only constructive way forward.

The way in which cancer affects the person will depend on what each Soul needs to derive from the experience.

All cases of miraculous recovery from terminal cancer will have entailed fundamental changes in the value systems of those affected. It could be said, then, that in order to heal, the sufferer had to become a *new person*.

No two cancers have identical roots.

The old way(s) of life effectively ended when the outbreak occurred. The outbreak occurred in order to end them, because allowing them to continue would not have been conducive to the needs of the Soul.

Cancer requires patience and discipline. The good person's disease, it is an option for Souls who work hard, aiming high. Cancer should never be seen as a punishment.

The Mechanics

Andreas Moritz, in his book <u>Cancer is not a Disease: It's a Survival Mechanism</u>, formulates the belief that cancer is a healing process, the purpose of which is to tackle another illness that could have led to death; and that an outbreak is the body's last desperate attempt to save itself.

He maintains, therefore, that it is not important to kill the cancer, but to eliminate the reason(s) that lead to it. Without eliminating the reasons, the cancer will always return.

Cancer works with the Soul along similar lines.

It protects the Soul from further damage, and it may be the last desperate attempt to save the Soul. The life of a Soul is under threat when it becomes unable to grow. Clinging to old values, after they become redundant, prevents the Soul from growing.

Every experience is relevant to the Souls of everyone who is affected by it. If a serious illness affects family members more than the sufferer, it was more relevant to them.

Souls are aware of what awaits them before incarnating, meaning that they know why they choose an experience.

A Soul will sacrifice not just one, but, if required, several lifetimes, to achieve an outcome that is important to all who are affected by it.

Cancer is not fundamentally different from any other serious illness; it is merely perceived differently, due to the stigma attached to it.

Except for a Soul with a mission, a pure Soul will not incarnate. A Soul also chooses parents, matching the experience they both need.

Family ties are not always based on a loving bond between similar Souls. A close encounter between contrasting Souls can often provide better opportunities for growth, as well as purification.

Healing

In order to heal, people need to accept responsibility for their own health; this also means working with the cancer, by asking pertinent questions, such as [1] What is this experience trying to teach me? [2] What new, or different, opportunities does it present?

A useful self-test is to imagine that you are someone else, who has to live with you, but can see and read every thought that you might have. If the idea feels uncomfortable, there may be work that you are expected to do.

Even when the thoughts become as pure as they can be, you may still have a task, and a lesson, to learn.

The process of learning, and transformation, takes time. In order to heal, you will have to learn your lesson from all presented angles, recognizing the correct answer, even when disguised in a new set of circumstances.

This is where you must learn to take notice of any theme that keeps repeating itself, for it is trying to teach you something that may only be unique, and personal, to you.

Do not expect others to know what to tell you.

This is where you must be entirely honest with yourself.

Spirit Guides are helping those who are guided to find answers through symbolism, visions, and premonitions.

It is important to take notice of these and to take care when interpreting them. To develop such abilities at a professional level requires years of experience, in addition to the gift; however, people usually come to sense the correct answer.

One must learn to open up to the advice that introduces a different slant, one that might prove to be far different than personally preferred, or generally adopted.

Serious life problems are triggered by clinging to values not worth pursuing; an illness, therefore, is an invitation to start with a review.

The success of a lifetime is not measured in years.

Unnecessary fears hamper healing, while the ability to think beyond matter helps to dissolve them. Attachment to possessions, others, and status, are chains.

Attachment does not heal, love does.

Andreas Moritz further believes that people have cancer without knowing, and that most (undiagnosed) cancers come and go by themselves, because the body's immune system had been designed to deal with them. Therefore, the most important factor in suppressing an outbreak is the body's own immune system.

A tumour may build around a part of the body which becomes a physical trigger of an outbreak. If possible, surgical removal of the affected parts reduces the amount of work the immune system will be required to do.

Healing By Nutrition

Nutrition is not only a source of energy, but also the building material from which the body constantly renews its different cells. Many degenerative diseases could be fended off with nutrition, meaning that nutrition can enable the repair in one part of the body without triggering new imbalances in another.

As much as is possible, the body needs to be kept free of obstructions, by removing possible gastric deposits, stones, and parasites.

Only a pure Soul will long for pure nutrition. The food that people are guided to eat, and are attracted to, matches their thoughts and their lifestyle. The body always reflects the person inside.

Conscious toxic intake remains attractive to many, just as there are cases when someone unwittingly develops an appetite for something unusual, and the substance happens to aid repair, of a kind, in their case.

There are diets (all strictly vegetarian), specific cleanses and herbal remedies which have assisted in the suppression of cancer in some cases, and there are books and centres which propagate them as cancer cures.

Different procedures suit different people (and different cancers).

A potent diet would have to be unique to each individual, because no two people have identical needs; similarly, no two people have the same DNA.

Even the nutrition which has been deemed good for the body today will not be good for it next week, because if the body heals, its requirements mutate, and a potent diet will have to lead the need.

Every bite the person eats matters, and will continue to affect the outcome. Food from the supermarket will not contain a sufficient enough concentration of active ingredients; quality food state supplements may be able to make up for potency.

A potent diet is unlikely to follow conventional recipes.

A variety of juices, dried or powdered plant products and herbal extracts, on the market are perceived as beneficial by some people.

Even with the most extreme of diets, the rule is not to take into the body food which tastes (looks or smells) revolting. Only the best, and most pure, nutrition can heal.

The degree to which the body heals is decided by progress made by the Soul; as such, it also is measured by how much the Soul grew, or became purified, through the experience.

The Soul's purpose is to achieve its goals, with incarnation being a means to an end. After all, self-preservation is the natural reaction of most physical forms of life.

Cancer Healing Summary via Soul Healing

[1] **A balanced attitude to life.** A judgmental or negative attitude to life encourages pathological processes in the body; blaming others is always counterproductive.

There is the need to acknowledge the existence of a positive side to every coin.

As well, everyone is expected to accept responsibility for their own life and the experience that it brings.

[2] **Working out the answer.** Understanding the *why me* can help one to regain emotional balance in new circumstances; one that can only serve to better assist in the designing of a healing plan.

[3] **Considering existing options and choosing a way forward.** Standing on an important cross-road, the person needs to realise *who* they really are.

He or she needs the strength, and the ability, to clearly formulate options, only following a positive direction which will become rewarding.

Cancer Healing Summary via Nutrition and Natural Supplements

[1] **A program to reduce toxic build up inside the body.** The procedures are based on the body's natural reactions to nutrition.

Cleansing the liver, bowels, and kidneys, are beneficial, in most cases, and to become a vegetarian is a requirement.

[2] **A unique, personalized diet.** Not just the type of food, but also the amount, and the way it is prepared, matter, and need to be taken into account.

[3] **Regular reviews of the diet.** Progress needs to be monitored, and the diet continually adjusted, to maintain an optimum potency level.

© http://www.dhaxem.com/dhaxem4.htm

Reprinted herein with permission (from Corascendea)

The Vicar of Christ, or *Vicarius Christi*, is a term, in keeping with the Papacy, that generally refers to the earthly representative of God or Christ; a most specific term (first appearing in the 5th century) used in reference to the Bishop of Rome (also known as the Pope). [94]

Interestingly, *Vicarius Filii Dei*, meaning Vicar of the Son of God, as in a physical representative, is a phrase that was first used in the medieval Donation of Constantine to refer to Saint Peter, a leader of the Early Christian Church who was regarded as the first Pope by the Catholic Church. [95] [96] [97]

In truth, this *forged* document was an imperial decree by which the Byzantine Emperor Constantine I *supposedly* transferred authority, over Rome and the western part of the Roman Empire, to the Pope.

---

[94] http://en.wikipedia.org/wiki/Vicar_of_Christ
[95] http://en.wikipedia.org/wiki/Vicarius_Filii_Dei
[96] http://en.wikipedia.org/wiki/Donation_of_Constantine
[97] http://en.wikipedia.org/wiki/Constantine_I

Constantine founded the City of Constantinople in 324 AD and yet the document *was said to have been* signed in 315 AD.

Fraudulently proclaimed to be the Vicar of Christ, this concocted document set forth a new precedent: the local bishop of Rome (aka the Pope) could now sanction *who* became king.

In 496 AD, Clovis I was the Merovingian king. [98] [99] It is said that he was of a special bloodline going back to Yeshua (Jesus), meaning the House of David.

In 496 AD, the Roman Church was *not* the dominant establishment, meaning that it was in competition with other groups (such as Arianism, for example).

It was King Clovis who, following his own conversion, was responsible for persuading much of Western Europe to convert to Christianity, thereby "firmly establishing

---

[98] 47th G grandfather (Catherine de Baillon connection) of the author.
[99] 49th G grandfather (Jacques Guéret dit Dumont connection) of the author.

Catholicism as the dominant religion within the Merovingian Kingdom, and saving the Church from almost certain collapse." [100]

The Church "agreed to pledge their allegiance to Clovis and promised that a new Holy Empire would be established under the auspices of the Merovingians." [101]

Having being proclaimed *Novus Constantinus* (emperor of a to-be-created Holy Roman Empire; a title which referenced the *New Constantine*), Clovis agreed to use his armies to crush any denominations that were in direct competition with the Roman Church.

When they granted him this title, Clovis "had no reason to doubt the sincerity of the Church, but unbeknownst to him, he had unwittingly become a pawn in a conspiracy for the Church to eventually seize control of his Kingdom, thereby establishing the Pope as the supreme ruler." [102]

---

[100] http://www.juneaustin.co.uk/merovingians.html
[101] Ibid.
[102] Ibid.

We are now going to fast forward to Dagobert II, son of Sigebert, grandson of Lothar and great grandson of Clovis I, also of the Merovingian line, born in 651 AD. It is said that because he was lax in serving the wishes of the Roman Church, thereby incurring "ecclesiastical displeasure," he was assassinated on December 23, 679 AD. [103] [104]

The successive Mayors of the Palace, namely, [1] Pépin II (c. 635 to 714; the first Duke of the Franks and father of Charles Martel, illegitimate son through his mistress, Alpaida), [2] Charles Martel (c. 686 to 741; grandfather of Charlemagne) and [3] Pépin III, also called Pépin the Short (c. 714 to 768; father of Charlemagne), continued to gain in personal power.

Pépin III was not satisfied with being Mayor; he wanted more. He wanted to be king. Coming to an arrangement with the Pope, by virtue of a spuriously forged document, none other than the Donation of Constantine (mysteriously discovered in 751 AD and supposedly written some 400

---

[103] http://doubleuoglobe.com/vol11/cn11-79.html

[104] http://www.juneaustin.co.uk/merovingians.html

years earlier), he was proclaimed king, leading to the removal, and imprisonment, of the true Merovingian king, Childeric III. [105] [106] [107] [108] [109]

As a means of legitimizing a claim, as was generally the case with royalty, it must also be shared that the maternal great grandmother of Charlemagne was Bertrada of Prüm, a Merovingian princess. It is thought that she was the daughter of Merovingian king Theuderic III (son of Clovis II and Bathilde) and Clotilde of Heristal.

As denoted by eminent chroniclers such as Hegesippus, Africanus and Eusebius, it was during the 1st century that the Messianic heirs (meaning the descendants of Jesus and his family) were hunted down and put to the sword by Roman Emperors; once the Roman Church was operative by the 4th century, the dynasty was forever doomed. [110]

---

[105] http://en.wikipedia.org/wiki/Pepin_II_the_Middle
[106] http://en.wikipedia.org/wiki/Charles_Martel
[107] http://en.wikipedia.org/wiki/Pepin_the_Short
[108] http://doubleuoglobe.com/vol11/cn11-79.html
[109] http://en.wikipedia.org/wiki/Childeric_III
[110] http://www.abovetopsecret.com/forum/thread138328/pg1

In retrospect, the Roman Church later directed specific brutal assaults, as in the Albigensian Crusades (which began in 1209) and Catholic Inquisitions, against all upholders and champions of the original concept of Grail kingship. [111]

In the Cathar language of old Provence, "a female elf was an albi (elbe or ylbi), and Albi was the name given to the main Cathar centre in Languedoc; this was in deference to the matrilinear heritage of the Grail dynasty, for the Cathars were supporters of the original *Albi*-gens: the Elven Bloodline which had descended through the Dragon Queens of yore, such as Lilith, Miriam, Bathsheba and Mary Magdalene. It was for this reason that, when Simon de Montfort and the armies of Pope Innocent III descended upon the region in 1209, it was called the Albigensian Crusade. Through some 35 years, tens of thousands of innocent people were slaughtered in this brutal campaign, all because the inhabitants of the region were champions of the original concept of Grail kingship, and against the

---

[111] http://www.abovetopsecret.com/forum/thread138328/pg1

pseudo-style of monarchy which had been implemented by the papal machine." [112]

The reason given "for the Church's campaign against the Cathars is generally that they were practitioners of a form of Gnostic Christianity," [113] a practice that was deemed heretical.

During the early formation of what would later come to be known as Christianity, church authorities (known as Fathers of the Church of Rome) exerted considerable influence (energy) in weeding out what they termed *false* doctrine.

While the writings of the Cathars have, for the most part, been destroyed, because of the doctrinal threat as perceived by the Papacy, there are a few texts that were preserved by their opponents.

The *Rituel Cathare de Lyon* provides us with a mere glimpse of the inner working of their faith.

---

[112] http://watch.pair.com/michael-archangel.html
[113] Ibid.

A Latin manuscript, *The Book of Two Principles*, kept in Florence, is "a translation made in 1260 from a work by the Cathar Jean de Lugio from Bergamo (written in 1230). The Latin translation, found in Prague in 1939, came from an anonymous treaty written in Languedoc at the beginning of the 13th century." [114] It is conceivable that the author may have been the Parfait Barthelemy of Carcassonne. This particular work outlines "the basis of a complete dualism that is reflected, in a veiled way, in the Holy Scriptures." [115]

There exists a widespread belief that the Knights Templar and the Cathars had a similar world-view, one that embraced a reverence of the Magdalene. It is known that the Templars "swore their oath to both Bethany and the Magdalene, showing that their *inside knowledge* prevented them from blindly following the edicts of Rome." [116]

---

[114] The Books by Gilles C. H.Nullens accessed on April 25, 2011 at http://www.nullens.org/catholics-heretics-and-heresy/part-1-the-cathars/1-2-introduction-to-the-cathar-religion-2/

[115] *Cathar Church and Doctrine* article accessed on April 25, 2011 at http://lespiraldelconeixement.com/dossier.cfm?lang=en&id=42

[116] Vayro, Ian Ross. (2007) *God Save Us From Religion* (page 187). Queensland, Australia: Joshua Books.

It could well be that they knew about the early Hebrew traditions dating back "to the time of Solomon when there was not only Yahweh, but also the Goddess Ashtoreth, or Astarte (as she was known in Mesopotamia)." [117]

Astarte was also the counterpart of Ishtar, the Assyrian and Babylonian goddess. Mentioned several times in the Old Testament, this divine feminine being "was openly worshipped by the Israelites until the 6th century BC when she was replaced by the single supreme male god of Jehovah." [118]

In reference to the Languedoc, word, of course, was sent "to the Pope that the Cathars were so inter-married into the local population of the region that it was impossible to identify who were Cathars and who weren't." [119]

When asked how the Crusaders would be able to discern the difference, the words uttered by Arnaud Amoury, the

---

[117] http://www.laughingowl.com/aleta/Knightsandsecret.htm
[118] Ibid.
[119] Vayro, Ian Ross. (2007) *God Save Us From Religion* (page 188). Queensland, Australia: Joshua Books.

Cistercian Abbott of Citeaux, were *Caedite eos ... Novit enim Dominus qui sunt eius ...* meaning *Kill them all. God will recognize his own.* [120] [121]

The Albigensian Heresy was "melded around the Jewish Messianic Bloodline of Jesus that Rome so desperately sought to suppress, and this goes a long way towards explaining the Church's fanatical, unprecedented savagery against the peaceful and non-threatening Cathars." [122]

The Languedoc was a "major source of Templar income and recruits. The Templars partly owed their great expansion in the region to the support of the nobility with whom they were in close alliance, the combination of nobles' land and Templar capital allowing the establishment of new communities and the development of previously

---

[120] http://en.wikipedia.org/wiki/Catharism

[121] http://www.cathar.info/120502_arnaud.htm

[122] Vayro, Ian Ross. (2007) *God Save Us From Religion* (page 188). Queensland, Australia: Joshua Books.

uncultivated territories.   Some of these Templar patrons were renowned Cathar supporters." [123]

Templar castles, houses and fortresses, "were thick on the ground in Languedoc, the heartland of Catharism. They provided refuge for Perfects during the Albigensian Crusade. Many of the noble families of the area who supported Catharism also had Templar Knights in the family.   Bertrand de Blanchefort, sixth Grand Master of the Templars, came from a Cathar family, and his descendants fought with the Cathars against the Albigensian Crusaders." [124]

When the Templars "last stronghold in the Holy Land came under Muslim control, they established their headquarters in southern France in an area now known as the Languedoc," [125] an area that was not officially part of France, given that

---

[123] http://bogomiltocathar.devhub.com/blog/588653-templars-and-cathars/
[124] http://www.medievalmysteries.com/Templars.html
[125] http://www.laughingowl.com/aleta/Knightsandsecret.htm

it was "an independent principality ruled by a handful of noble families." [126]

Aside from ideological disputes, the fast spread of Catharism in the 13th century "meant a painfully growing loss of land and influence. If allowed to continue, the impact of Catharism would have re-defined the fabric of medieval society. To protect the existing power base, the inquisition had been formed to get rid of the Cathars, by means of their complete genocide. Their democracy and Christ-like lifestyles had been considered an example too dangerous to allow even a trace of it to remain. The Christian Church, to date, proudly claims the brutal murder of unarmed Cathar men, women and children whose "fault" had been their sincere desire to live according to the values of Christ, to be its most significant victory." [127]

The traditional death toll, in a war against the Cathars, a brutal genocide inflicted on a peaceable Christian people, paragons of spirituality and virtue, has been cited as one

---

[126] http://www.laughingowl.com/aleta/Knightsandsecret.htm
[127] http://www.dhaxem.com/the_cathars.htm

million, over the course of forty years, as per the following sources: [1] John M. Robertson, *A Short History of Christianity* (London: Watts, 1902) p. 254; [2] Christopher Brookmyre, *Not the End of the World* (New York: Grove Press, 1998) p. 39; [3] Max Dimont, *Jews, God, and History* (New York: Penguin, 1994) p. 225; [4] Dizerega Gus, *Pagans & Christians: The Personal Spiritual Experience* (St. Paul, MN: Llewellyn, 2001) p. 195; [5] Helen Ellerbe, *The Dark Side of Christian History* (Orlando, FL: Morningstar & Lark, 1995) p. 74, and [6] Michael Newton, *Holy Homicide* (Port Townsend, WA: Loompanics Unlimited, 1998) p. 117. [128]

Albigensian Crusade [129]

---

[128] http://necrometrics.com/pre1700a.htm

[129] http://en.wikipedia.org/wiki/Albigensian_Crusade

Albigensian Crusade: Online Reference Book for Medieval Studies [130]

Andrew Gough's Arcadia [131]

Battle of Montségur [132]

Brethren Persecuted, Part 1 [133]

Brethren Persecuted, Part 2 [134]

Brethren Persecuted, Part 3 [135]

Bogomils and Cathars [136]

Cathar Castles [137]

Cathar Honour [138]

Catharism [139] [140]

---

[130] http://www.the-orb.net/textbooks/crusade/albig.html
[131] http://www.andrewgough.co.uk/
[132] http://balisunset.hubpages.com/hub/Battle-of-Montsegur
[133] http://blog.templarhistory.com/2010/08/brethren-persecuted-part-1/
[134] http://blog.templarhistory.com/2010/08/brethren-persecuted-part-2/
[135] http://blog.templarhistory.com/2010/08/brethren-persecuted-%e2%80%93-part-3/
[136] http://www.nullens.org/an-outsiders-view-of-freemasonry/part-a-old-craft/a-6-bogomils-and-cathars/
[137] http://www.catharcastles.info/
[138] http://www.dhaxem.com/data/handt/Cathar_Honour.pdf
[139] http://en.wikipedia.org/wiki/Catharism
[140] http://dolphyns.free.fr/English_Version/albigensians.htm

Catharism: Should Basic Christianity Be Revived? [141]

Catharism Spirituality [142]

Catharist Credentes, Part 1 [143]

Catharist Credentes, Part 2 [144]

Cathar Fotresses of the Languedoc [145]

Cathar Martyrdom: The Cathar View [146]

Cathars [147] [148] [149]

Cathars: A Medieval Tragedy [150]

Cathars and Cathar Beliefs in the Languedoc [151]

---

[141] http://angiejardine.hubpages.com/hub/Catharism-should-basic-Christianity-be-revived

[142] http://www.john.atalant.com/15%20pearls%20of%20Catharism.html

[143] http://bogomiltocathar.devhub.com/blog/534574-catharist-credentes-i/

[144] http://bogomiltocathar.devhub.com/blog/534573-catharist-credentes-ii/

[145] http://members.virtualtourist.com/m/a05dc/1eabc/

[146] http://www.dhaxem.com/data/handt/Cathar_Martyrdom.pdf

[147] http://www.geni.com/projects/Cathars

[148] http://www.mysticmissal.org/cathars.htm

[149] http://bogomiltocathar.devhub.com/blog/534555-cathars/

[150] http://www.computours.net/cathar/

[151] http://www.cathar.info/

Cathars and Reincarnation [152]

Cathars Recorded as Heretics [153]

Cathar Texts and Rituals [154]

Ceremonies: The Consolamentum [155]

Christianity and Its Persecution of the Cathars [156]

Church to Inquisition, Part 1 [157]

Church to Inquisition, Part 2 [158]

Citadels of Vertigo and the Ethics of Desire [159]

City of Béziers Captured By Crusaders [160]

Dhaxem: The Cathar Testament [161]

---

[152] http://www.innervision.com/mysteries/cathars.html
[153] http://www.chinstitute.org/index.php/eras/medieval/cathars/
[154] http://www.gnosis.org/library/cathtx.htm
[155] http://www.cathar.info/12011001_consolamentum.htm
[156] http://www.heretication.info/_cathars.html
[157] http://bogomiltocathar.devhub.com/blog/590270-church-to-inquisition-i/
[158] http://bogomiltocathar.devhub.com/blog/590271-church-to-inquisition-ii/
[159] http://textualities.net/morelle-smith/citadels-of-vertigo-and-the-ethics-of-desire/
[160] http://burnpit.us/2010/07/city-b%C3%A9ziers-captured-crusaders-kill-them-all-god-will-know-his-own
[161] http://www.dhaxem.com/index.php

Et in Arcadia Ego [162]

God of Love and Bon Hommes [163]

Gordon Napier History Blog [164]

History of the Albigensian Heresy [165]

Inquisition Deux [166]

Kill Them All [167]

Land of the Cathars [168]

Land of the Cathars [169]

Languedoc [170]

Legend of the Cathars [171]

---

[162] http://www.et-in-arcadia-ego.com/html/Arcadia0B.php
[163] http://www.john.atalant.com/God%20of%20Love.html
[164] http://gordonnapierhistory.blogspot.com/2010/04/my-first-book-rise-and-fall-of-knights.html
[165] http://bogomiltocathar.devhub.com/blog/534622-history-of-the-albigensian-heresy/
[166] http://bogomiltocathar.devhub.com/blog/534557-inquisition-deux/
[167] http://stephenosheaonline.com/hits-KillThemAll.html
[168] http://www.trans4mind.com/counterpoint/index-esoteric/shepherd4.shtml
[169] http://www.panoccitania.com/cathars.html
[170] http://flagspot.net/flags/fr-lr.html
[171] http://gnosistraditions.faithweb.com/mont.html

Le Pays Cathare [172]

Manecheism, Catharism and Freemasonry [173]

Massacre at Béziers [174]

Massacre at Montségur: A History of the Albigensian Crusade [175]

Montségur [176] [177]

Montségur and Carcassonne [178]

Montségur and Its Mysteries [179]

Montségur and The Cathars (Peter Vronsky) [180]

---

[172] http://about-france.com/tourism/cathar-country.htm
[173] http://www.eleggua.com/Objects/Koulias-Manicheism,_Catharism_and_Freemasonry.html
[174] http://en.wikipedia.org/wiki/Massacre_at_B%C3%A9ziers
[175] http://bogomiltocathar.devhub.com/blog/category/albigensian-crusade/
[176] http://www.catharcastles.info/montsegur.php?key=montsegur
[177] http://www.catharmaiden.com/homepage/pilgrimage/15montsegur.htm
[178] http://www.dhaxem.com/data/articles/Montsegur_and_Carcassonne.pdf
[179] http://writingaboutrenneslechateau.blog4ever.com/blog/lire-article-322270-2550617-montsegur_and_its_mysteries.html
[180] http://www.russianbooks.org/montsegur.htm

Montségur Photo Tour [181]

Montségur: The Last Bastion of the Cathars [182]

Mysteries of Southern France [183]

Mystery of the Cathars [184]

Names of Montségur Martyrs [185]

Persecution of the Cathars [186]

Political Background of the Cathar Genocide [187]

Primary Sources of the Albigensian Crusades [188]

Rebellion and Resistance: The History of Languedoc [189]

Secrets of the Cathars [190] [191]

---

[181] http://gofrance.about.com/od/photogalleries/ss/montsegurtour.htm
[182] http://www.valeriebarrow.com/jehanne-darc/travels-to-sacred-places/montsegur-the-last-bastion-of-the-cathars.html
[183] http://www.innervision.com/mysteries/cathars.html
[184]

http://www.john.atalant.com/Mystery%20of%20the%20Cathars.html
[185] http://www.cathar.info/1211b_martyrdom.htm
[186] http://www.badnewsaboutchristianity.com/gbe_cathars.htm
[187] http://www.dhaxem.com/data/handt/Catharism_-_Political_Background.pdf
[188] http://www.crusades-encyclopedia.com/primarysourcesalbigensiancrusade.html
[189] http://www.creme-de-languedoc.com/Languedoc/history.php
[190] http://www.bibliotecapleyades.net/esp_autor_whenry04.htm

Simon de Montfort [192]

Simon of Montfort and the Campaign of 1210, Part 1 [193]

Simon of Montfort and the Campaign of 1210, Part 2 [194]

Templars and Cathars [195]

The Albigensian Crusade [196]

The Albigensian Crusade: People, Coinage, Places [197]

The Albigensian Crusaders [198]

The Albigensian Crusades [199]

---

[191]

http://www.hiddenmysteries.org/author/henry/secrets_of_the_cathars.pdf

[192]

http://en.wikipedia.org/wiki/Simon_de_Montfort,_5th_Earl_of_Leicester

[193] http://bogomiltocathar.devhub.com/blog/534580-simon-of-montfort-and-the-campaign-of-1210-part-i/

[194] http://bogomiltocathar.devhub.com/blog/534578-simon-of-montfort-and-the-campaign-of-1210-part-ii/

[195] http://bogomiltocathar.devhub.com/blog/588653-templars-and-cathars/

[196] http://www.halexandria.org/dward220.htm

[197] http://home.eckerd.edu/~oberhot/cathar.htm

[198] http://bogomiltocathar.devhub.com/blog/534615-albigensian-crusade-the-crusaders-part-i/

[199] http://xenophongroup.com/montjoie/albigens.htm

The Buzzard: A Short Historical Piece [200]

The Campaign of 1209, Part 1 [201]

The Campaign of 1209, Part 2 [202]

The Campaign of 1209, Part 3 [203]

The Cathar Epic [204]

The Cathar Fortresses [205]

The Cathar Genocide [206]

The Cathar Mantrum [207]

The Cathar Martyrs: Ville Béziers [208]

The Cathar Prophecy of 1244 AD [209]

---

[200] http://www.computours.net/cathar/buzzard.htm
[201] http://bogomiltocathar.devhub.com/blog/534606-albigensian-crusadethe-campaign-of-1209-part-i/
[202] http://bogomiltocathar.devhub.com/blog/534605-the-campaign-of-1209-part-ii/
[203] http://bogomiltocathar.devhub.com/blog/534597-the-campaign-of-1209-part-iii-august-september-1209/
[204] http://www.francemonthly.com/n/0905/index.php#article3
[205] http://garrenshay.blogspot.com/2011/10/cathar-fortresses.html
[206] http://www.dhaxem.com/data/handt/Cathar_Genocide.pdf
[207] http://www.wholisticworldvision.org/inspirations.html
[208] http://cathar-martyr.tripod.com/beziers.html
[209] http://beingatruehuman.wordpress.com/2010/01/15/the-cathar-prophecy-of-1244-ad-the-fountain/

The Cathars [210] [211] [212] [213]

The Cathars, Part 1 [214]

The Cathars, Part 2 [215]

The Cathars and the Albigensian Crusade [216]

The Cathars: Chronology of Events [217]

The Cathars in Languedoc [218]

The Cathars: The Struggle for, and of, a New Church [219]

---

[210] http://www.ancientquest.com/embark/cathars.html

[211] http://www.ariegeaudeforum.com/index.php?option=com_content&view=article&id=750:the-cathars&catid=337:history-of-our-region

[212] http://www.theblackboxspeaks.org/cathars.html

[213] http://s155239215.onlinehome.us/turkic/50Religion/CatharsEn.htm

[214] http://www.midihideaways.com/journal/cathars.html

[215] http://www.midihideaways.com/journal/catharsII.html

[216] http://www.military-history.us/2011/08/the-cathars-and-the-albigensian-crusade/

[217] http://www.cathar.info/1202b_chronolgy.htm

[218] http://www.golanguedoc.com/best-languedoc-sites/cathars-in-languedoc.html

[219] http://www.philipcoppens.com/catharism.html
http://www.dhaxem.com/data/handt/The_Struggles_for_a_New_Church.pdf

The Cathars: Trials and Tribulations in the Languedoc [220]

The Church's War on The Cathars [221] [222]

The Consolamentum [223]

The Crusade Against The Cathars [224] [225]

The Crusades and Inquisition [226]

The Enigma of the Cathars, Part 1 [227]

The Enigma of the Cathars, Part 2 [228]

---

[220]

http://www.rosicrucian.org/publications/digest/digest2_2011/04_web/
08_anderson/08_anderson_112311.pdf

[221]

http://www.dhaxem.com/data/handt/The_Church_War_on_the_Cathar
s.pdf

[222] http://www.bibliotecapleyades.net/esp_cataros_07.htm

[223] http://www.refractum.com/garden-eden/the-consolamentum.html

[224] http://mescladis.free.fr/ANGLAIS/pages%20html/crusade.htm

[225]

http://www.doorzicht.eventwebsitebuilder.com/crusadesagainstcathars.
html

[226] http://www.netplaces.com/gnostic-gospels/consequences-of-
heresy/the-crusades-and-inquisition.htm

[227] http://templeofpegasus.blogspot.com/2008/08/enigma-of-cathars-
part-one.html

[228] http://templeofpegasus.blogspot.com/2008/08/enigma-of-cathars-
part-two.html

The Enigma of the Cathars, Part 3 [229]

The Enigma of the Cathars, Part 4 [230]

The Enigma of the Cathars, Part 5 [231]

The Enigma of the Cathars, Epilogue [232]

The Fire of Love [233]

The Forgotten Kingdom: The Tragedy of the Cathars [234]

The Great Mysteries of the Languedoc [235]

The Hidden History of The Secret Church [236]

The Knights Templar: The Cathar Connection [237]

---

[229] http://templeofpegasus.blogspot.com/2008/08/enigma-of-cathars-part-three.html

[230] http://templeofpegasus.blogspot.com/2008/09/enigma-of-cathars-part-four.html

[231] http://templeofpegasus.blogspot.com/2008/09/enigma-of-cathars-part-five.html

[232] http://templeofpegasus.blogspot.com/2008/09/enigma-of-cathars-epilogue.html

[233] http://www.john.atalant.com/The%20Fire%20of%20Love.html

[234] http://music.douban.com/review/2860158/

[235] http://www.languedocmysteries.info/

[236]

http://www.gnostic.info/mikhael_Hidden%20History%20Secret%20Church.html

[237] http://www.dhaxem.com/data/handt/Knights_Templar.pdf

The Land of the Cathars [238]

The Legend of the Cathars [239]

The Lessons of the Albigensian Crusades [240]

The Magdalene of the Heretics, Part 1 [241]

The Magdalene of the Heretics, Part 2 [242]

The Martyrdom of the Cathars [243]

The Medieval Inquisition in the Languedoc [244]

The Medieval Roman Inquisition [245]

---

[238] http://www.midicanal.fr/catharegb.html

[239] http://www.bibliotecapleyades.net/esp_cataros_03.htm

[240] http://webzine.thesocialedge.com/columns/the-lessons-of-the-albigensian-crusade/

[241] http://www.templeofmysteries.com/mary-magdalene/the-magdalene-of-the-heretics-part-i.php

[242] http://www.templeofmysteries.com/mary-magdalene/the-magdalene-of-the-heretics-part-ii.php

[243] http://www.trekearth.com/gallery/Europe/France/South/Midi-Pyrenees/Montsegur/photo286675.htm

[244] http://www.cathar.info/1209_inquisition.htm

[245]

http://www.dhaxem.com/data/handt/Medieval_Roman_Inquisition.pdf

The Path of Shadows: The Story of Montségur [246]

The Perfect Heresy [247]

The Perfect Heretics [248]

The Pure Ones [249]

The Rise of Heresies and Catholic Responses [250]

The Secret of the Tarot [251]

The Siege of Carcassonne (August 1209) [252]

The Storm of Béziers [253] [254]

The Story of the Cathars [255]

---

[246] http://www.aubergemontsegur.com/Montsegur/PathShadows/path_of_shadows.htm

[247] http://www.briancreese.co.uk/cathars.htm

[248] http://www.playbackarts.co.uk/meryfela/perfect.htm

[249] http://www.bibliotecapleyades.net/esp_cataros_06.htm

[250] http://www.gutenberg-e.org/maclehose/appendix2.html

[251] http://www.thesecretofthetarot.com/

[252] http://bogomiltocathar.devhub.com/blog/534603-the-siege-of-carcassonne-1-15-august-1209/

[253] http://www.warandgamemsw.com/blog/529778-the-storm-of-bziers/

[254] http://bogomiltocathar.devhub.com/blog/category/albigensian-crusade/page-2/

[255] http://www.cathar22.com/page23.html

The Templars, Cathars and Mary Magdalene [256]

The Tragic Fate of the Cathars [257]

The Treasure of the Knights Templar, Part 1 [258]

The Treasure of the Knights Templar, Part 2 [259]

The Voice of the Cathars, Part 1 (by Louis Khourey) [260]

The Voice of the Cathars, Part 2 (by Louis Khourey) [261]

The Voice of the Cathars, Part 3 (by Louis Khourey) [262]

The Walls of Carcassonne [263]

The Wooden Book of Montségur [264]

Toulouse: Sieges [265]

---

[256] http://dashinvaine.co.uk/magdalen%20page.htm
[257] http://www.netplaces.com/gnostic-gospels/consequences-of-heresy/the-tragic-fate-of-the-cathars.htm
[258] http://bogomiltocathar.devhub.com/blog/534619-the-treasure-of-the-knights-templar-part-i/
[259] http://bogomiltocathar.devhub.com/blog/534618-the-treasure-of-the-knights-templar-part-ii/
[260] http://tatfoundation.org/forum2001-06.htm
[261] http://tatfoundation.org/forum2001-07.htm
[262] http://tatfoundation.org/forum2001-08.htm
[263] http://www.kellscraft.com/Navarre/OldNavarreCh09.html
[264] http://www.philipcoppens.com/woodenbook.html
[265] http://bogomiltocathar.devhub.com/blog/700052-toulouse-sieges/

Wars against the Cathars of the Languedoc (by Voltaire) [266]

What Makes a Cathar? [267]

Who Are The Cathars? [268]

Zarathushtra, Mani, and the Cathars [269]

---

[266] http://www.languedoc-france.info/articles/t_voltairecathars.htm
[267] http://www.dhaxem.com/data/handt/What_makes_a_Cathar.pdf
[268] http://www.sullivan-county.com/id2/gnostic_files/cather.htm
[269] http://san.beck.org/GPJ8-ManiandCathars.html

We know that the Albigensian Crusades were aimed at eradicating a population, merely because they *did not conform* to the traditions of the Roman Catholic Church. We also know that it was a conflict that "quickly devolved into a political war of conquest and land seizure." [270]

With Catharism threatening "the very existence, ubiquity and legitimacy of the Catholic Church," [271] this was naught but political and religious genocide at its best.

The cycle of atrocities had its beginnings at Casseneuil, a town that was controlled by the Bishop of Agen's own brother, Hugh. The town was spared in exchange for the handing over of Cathar heretics, all of whom refused to recant their faith. [272] [273]

---

[270] http://www.deremilitari.org/2011/03/the-albigensian-crusade-a-comparative-military-study-1209-1218/
[271] Ibid.
[272] http://bogomilcahar.blogspot.com/2009/03/campaign-of-1209-part-ii.html

It was early in July 1209 that Simon de Montfort "captured the hilltop village of Servian, prior to going to Béziers." [274]

On July 22, 1209, the feast day of the Magdalene, 20,000 were slaughtered at Béziers, situated on the western banks of the Orb River, regardless of rank, age or sex, a town in which there lived but 222 Cathars. [275] [276] [277] [278] It was demanded that the town elders give up the Cathars; they refused.

All were butchered within the Roman-Gothic Église de La Madeleine (Church of Mary Magdalene) ... *a massacre without parallel in European history*, according to Historian H. C. Lea in his book, The Inquisition in the Middle Ages. [279] The town was also looted and torched. [280]

---

[273] http://www.katemosse.co.uk/?page_id=580

[274] http://xenophongroup.com/montjoie/albigens.htm

[275] http://www.ebooks.com/273988/the-cathars/martin-sean/

[276] http://www.katemosse.co.uk/?page_id=576

[277] http://www.katemosse.co.uk/?page_id=582

[278] http://xenophongroup.com/montjoie/albigens.htm

[279] http://webzine.thesocialedge.com/columns/the-lessons-of-the-albigensian-crusade/

[280] http://www.catharcastles.info/beziers.php?key=beziers

Next came the beautiful walled city of Carcassonne, besieged from August 1 to August 15, 1209. [281] Knowing that it would be needed as a base of operations, it escaped the fiery fate of Béziers. [282] [283]

Raymond Roger Trencavel was Viscount of Béziers as well as Carcassonne; his cities were deliberately targeted by the Crusaders, mainly because the Count of Toulouse had joined the Crusade, gaining immunity for his own lands. [284] Raymond Roger was taken prisoner and the inhabitants of Carcassonne were expelled.

The lesson taken from Béziers had been "that massacres risked the total destruction of the city, including the loss of all loot by fire." [285] As a result, Arnaud Amaury, the papal legate, wrote to the pope, Innocent III, "to explain why, on this occasion, no one had been killed. It is at this stage that

---

[281] http://www.catharcastles.info/carcassonne.php?key=carcassonne
[282] http://webzine.thesocialedge.com/columns/the-lessons-of-the-albigensian-crusade/
[283] http://www.katemosse.co.uk/?page_id=578
[284] http://www.catharcastles.info/carcassonne.php?key=carcassonne
[285] Ibid.

Simon de Montfort was appointed to hold Raymond Roger's territories." [286]

It was in March 1210 that Simon de Montfort took "the citadel of Bram after three days of siege. He then had the nose and upper lip cut from each prisoner, and had their eyes gauged out. For one, he left one eye so that he could guide this lamentable cohort across the country to seek refuge at Lastours." [287] [288]

Surrendered to the Crusaders on July 22, 1210, it was in Minerve, the site of a ten week siege by Simon de Montfort, that Cathars "took refuge after the massacre of Béziers in 1209. Guilhem saved the villagers, but he could not save the Cathars who had taken refuge in the town." [289] Some 180 Parfaits were burned to death at the insistence of Catholic Church leaders." [290] [291]

---

[286] http://www.catharcastles.info/carcassonne.php?key=carcassonne
[287] http://www.castlesandmanorhouses.com/p.php?key=bram
[288] http://xenophongroup.com/montjoie/albigens.htm
[289] http://www.catharcastles.info/minerve.php?key=minerve
[290] Ibid.
[291] http://www.computours.net/cathar/

Failing to conquer Lastours, Simon de Montfort turned his attention to Termes, which "fell after a siege lasting four months, from August to November 1210, the hardest siege of the first period of the Albigensian Crusade." [292]

In March 1211, Lavaur (the seat of the Cathar Bishop of Toulouse) was besieged by Simon de Montfort. The town "fell on May 3, 1211, following which the French Catholic Crusaders excelled even themselves in cruelty and disregard for the accepted rules of war." [293] [294]

There were at least 400 Cathar parfaits living in Lavaur, all of whom were burned alive. The head of the local garrison and 80 of his knights were hanged, with his much loved sister, thrown into a well, while still alive, wherein they heaped stones on top of her. [295] [296]

---

[292] http://www.catharcastles.info/termes.php?key=termes
[293] http://www.catharcastles.info/lavaur.php?key=lavaur
[294] http://www.katemosse.co.uk/?page_id=580
[295] http://webzine.thesocialedge.com/columns/the-lessons-of-the-albigensian-crusade/
[296] http://www.katemosse.co.uk/?page_id=580

The first siege of Toulouse took place from June 16 to June 29, 1211, without success. [297]

Simon de Montfort and his French Crusader army were holed up at Castelnaudary, with the first siege taking place on September 1211. Raymond VI, the Count of Toulouse, along with his allies, the Count of Foix and Savaric de Mauléon, were the individuals who were besieging Castelnaudary. [298]

It was also in September 1211, during the Battle of Saint-Martin LaLande, that Simon de Montfort was victorious against Raymond VI, the Count of Toulouse, and his strongest ally, Raymond Roger, the Count of Foix.

The Battle of Muret (which took place on September 13, 1213), was one in which Simon de Montfort was successful in taking the City of Toulouse. After taking over the city, he was quick to force the inhabitants to demolish their defensive walls so that the city would be indefensible; after

---

[297] http://www.catharcastles.info/toulouse.php?key=toulouse
[298] http://www.catharcastles.info/castelnaudary.php?key=castelnaudry

which he installed himself, along with a garrison, in Raymond's palace, the Château Narbonnais. [299]

In 1214, Casseneuil bore the brunt of the crusade, until it fell in the last great crusader military victory. [300]

Beginning in early September 1216, and lasting until October, there was an uprising against the occupying forces. September 12, 1217, saw Raymond VI, Count of Toulouse, re-entering the city, trapping the family of Simon de Montfort in the Château. Every man, woman and capable child worked to rebuild the walls of the city, from sun up to sun down, achieving what seemed an impossible task; making the place defensible before Simon's return. [301]

It was the castle of Beaucaire that saw some of the most impressive action in the crusade against the Cathars of the Languedoc, including the turning point in the military career

---

[299] http://www.catharcastles.info/toulouse.php?key=toulouse

[300] http://bogomilcahar.blogspot.com/2009/03/campaign-of-1209-part-ii.html

[301] Ibid.

of the Crusade leader Simon de Montfort, one which marked the beginning of the end. [302]

There was a second siege of Toulouse, lasting from September 13, 1217 to July 22, 1218, without success. During this siege, Simon de Montfort died, when, on June 25, 1218, he was hit in the head by a stone from a trebuchet,[303] to the great rejoicing of the citizens of Toulouse, and the whole of the Languedoc region. [304]

There was also a third siege of Toulouse, conducted by Prince Louis (the future King Louis IX) lasting from June 16, 1219 to August 1, 1219; once again, without success. [305]

It was in 1219 that Marmonde, a town of some 7,000 people, was razed and set alight. [306] [307] A second siege, took place at Castelnaudary, between July 1220 and March 1221. [308]

---

[302] http://www.catharcastles.info/beaucaire.php?key=beaucaire
[303] http://en.wikipedia.org/wiki/Trebuchet
[304] http://www.catharcastles.info/toulouse.php?key=toulouse
[305] Ibid.
[306] http://www.serenitytravels.com/cathar_missions.html
[307] http://www.catharcastles.info/marmande.php?key=marmande
[308] http://www.catharcastles.info/castelnaudary.php?key=castelnaudry

It was 1229 before the *Treaty of Paris* ended the Albigensian Crusades.

In 1233, the Inquisition was sent forth, by Pope Gregory IX, to uproot Catharism in the Languedoc.

On March 16, 1244, the citadel at Montségur, was defeated and 215 Cathars were burned at the stake; they refused to recant their faith. [309] [310] [311]

Quéribus, the last Cathar castle, was seized in August 1255, formally ending the Crusade. [312] [313]

The last known burning of a person who professed Cathar beliefs (William Beliaste) occurred in Corbières, present-day Switzerland, in 1321. [314]

---

[309] http://www.dailykos.com/story/2009/05/03/727514/-History-for-Kossacks:-Europes-First-Police-State
[310] http://www.katemosse.co.uk/?page_id=584
[311] http://www.katemosse.co.uk/?page_id=582
[312] http://www.dailykos.com/story/2009/05/03/727514/-History-for-Kossacks:-Europes-First-Police-State
[313] http://www.catharcastles.info/queribus.php?key=queribus
[314] http://en.wikipedia.org/wiki/Albigensian_Crusade

$\mathscr{Bibliography}$

CATHARS AND CATHARISM

Arnold, John. (2001) *Inquisition and Power: Catharism and the Confessing Subject in Medieval Languedoc.*

Barber, Malcolm. (2000) *The Cathars: Dualist Heretics in Languedoc in the High Middle Ages.*

Burnham, Sophy. (2002) *The Treasure of Montségur: A Novel of the Cathars.*

Costen, Michael. (1997) *The Cathars and The Albigensian Crusade.*

Cowper, Marcus and Dennis, Peter. (2006) *Cathar Castles: Fortresses of the Albigensian Crusade 1209-1300.*

Craney, Glen. (2008) *The Fire and the Light: A Novel of the Cathars and the Lost Teachings of Christ.*

Douzet, André. (2006) *The Wandering of the Grail: The Cathars, the Search for the Grail, and the Discovery of Egyptian Relics in the French Pyrenees.*

Guirdham, Arthur. (2004) *The Cathars & Reincarnation.*

Guirdham, Arthur. (2004) *We Are One Another.*

Guirdham, Arthur. (2004) *The Lake and The Castle.*

Hughes, Nita. (2003) *Past Recall: When Love and Wisdom Transcend Time.*

Hughes, Nita. (2006) *The Cathar Legacy.*

Lambert, Malcolm D. (1998) *The Cathars.*

Markale, Jean. (2003) *Montségur and The Mystery of the Cathars.*

Martin, Sean. (2004) *The Cathars: The Most Successful Heresy of the Middle Ages.*

Mattingly, Alan. (2005) *Walking in the Cathar Region: Cathar Castles of South West France.*

Moerland, Bram. (2009) *The Cathars*.

Oldenbourg, Zoe. (2006) *Massacre at Montsegur: A History of the Albigensian Crusade*.

O'Shea, Stephen (2001) *The Perfect Heresy: The Revolutionary Life and Death of the Medieval Cathars*.

Stoyanov, Yuri. (2000) *The Other God: Dualist Religions from Antiquity to the Cathar Heresy*.

Strayer, Joseph. (1992) *The Albigensian Crusades*.

Vasilev, Georgi. (2007) *Heresy and the English Reformation: Bogomil-Cathar Influence on Wycliffe, Langland, Tyndale and Milton*.

Weis, Rene. (2002) *The Yellow Cross: The Story of the Last Cathar's Rebellion Against the Inquisition, 1290-1329*.

HERBOLOGY

Castleman, Michael. (2010) *The New Healing Herbs: The Essential Guide to More Than 125 of Nature's Most Potent Herbal Remedies*.

HOLY BLOODLINE, HOLY GRAIL

Andrews, Richard. (1996) *The Tomb of God: The Body of Jesus and The Solution To A 2,000 Year Old Mystery.*

Arimathea, Joseph of. (1999) *The Book of The Holy Grail.*

Baigent, Michael; Leigh, Richard and Lincoln, Henry. (2004) *Holy Blood, Holy Grail.*

Bradley, Michael. (1996) *Holy Grail Across the Atlantic: The Secret History of Canadian Discovery and Exploration.*

Bradley, Michael. (1998) *Grail Knights of North America: On the Trail of the Grail Legacy in Canada and the United States.*

Bradley, Michael. (2005) *Swords at Sunset: Last Stand of North America's Grail Knights.*

Emerys, Chevalier. (2007) *Revelation of the Holy Grail.*

Francke, Sylvia. (2007) *The Tree of Life and The Holy Grail: Ancient and Modern Spiritual Paths and the Mystery of Rennes-le-Château.*

Gardiner, Philip and Osborn, Gary. (2006) *The Serpent Grail: The Truth Behind the Holy Grail, the Philosopher's Stone and the Elixir of Life.*

Gardner, Laurence. (2000) *Genesis of the Grail Kings: The Explosive Story of Genetic Cloning of and the Ancient Bloodline of Jesus.*

Gardner, Laurence. (2001) *Bloodline of the Holy Grail: The Hidden Lineage of Jesus Revealed.*

Gardner, Laurence. (2006) *The Magdalene Legacy: The Jesus and Mary Bloodline Conspiracy.*

Gardner, Laurence. (2008) *The Grail Enigma: The Hidden Heirs of Jesus and Mary Magdalene.*

Johnson, Bettye. (2005) *Secrets of the Magdalene Scrolls: The Forbidden Truth of the Life and Times of Mary Magdalene.*

Johnson, Bettye. (2007) *Mary Magdalene, Her Story.*

Lincoln, Henry. (2004) *The Holy Place: Sauniere and the Decoding of the Mystery of Rennes-le-Château.*

Miles, Rosalind. (2002) *The Child of the Holy Grail.*

Ortenberg, Veronica. (2006) *In Search of The Holy Grail.*

Phillips, Graham. (2001) *The Marian Conspiracy: The Hidden Truth About the Holy Grail, The Real Father of Christ.*

Pinkham, Mark Amaru. (2004) *Guardians of the Holy Grail: The Knights Templar, John the Baptist, and the Water of Life.*

Simmans, Graham. (2007) *Jesus After The Crucifixion: From Jerusalem to Rennes-le-Château.*

Twyman, Tracy R. (2004) *The Merovingian Mythos and the Mystery of Rennes-le-Château.*

Wallace-Murphy, Tim and Hopkins, Marilyn. (2000) *Rosslyn: Guardian of the Secret of the Holy Grail.*

Wallace-Murphy, Tim; Simmons, Graham and Hopkins, Marilyn. (2000) *Rex Deus: The True Mystery of Rennes-le-Château.*

Young, John K. (2003) *Sacred Sites of the Knights Templar: Ancient Astronomers and Freemasons at Stonehenge, Rennes-le-Château and Santiago de Compostela.*

KNIGHTS TEMPLAR

Addison, Charles G. (1997) *History of the Knights Templar.*

Barber, Malcolm. (1993) *The Trial of the Templars.*

Bradley, Michael. (1996) *Holy Grail Across the Atlantic: The Secret History of Canadian Discovery and Exploration.*

Bradley, Michael. (1998) *Grail Knights of North America: On the Trail of the Grail Legacy in Canada and the United States.*

Bradley, Michael. (2005) *Swords at Sunset: Last Stand of North America's Grail Knights.*

Bradley, Michael. (2008) *The Secrets about the Freemasons.*

Butler, Alan and Dafoe, Stephen. (1999) *The Knights Templar Revealed: The Secrets of the Cistercian Legacy.*

Butler, Alan and Dafoe, Stephen. (2006) *The Warriors and the Bankers: A History of the Knights Templar from 1307 to the Present.*

Dafoe, Stephen. (2007) *Nobly Born: An Illustrated History of The Knights Templar.*

Dafoe, Stephen. (2008) *The Compass and the Cross: A History of the Masonic Knights Templar.*

Gardner, Laurence. (2007) *The Shadow of Solomon: The Lost Secret of the Freemasons Revealed.*

Knight, Christopher and Lomas, Robert. (2001) *The Hiram Key: Pharaohs, Freemasonry, and the Discovery of the Secret Scrolls of Jesus.*

Knight, Christopher and Lomas, Robert. (2001) *Second Messiah: Templars, the Turin Shroud and the Great Secret of Freemasonry.*

Mann, William. (2004) *The Knights Templar in the New World: How Henry Sinclair Brought the Grail to Acadia.*

Mann, William. (2006) *The Templar Meridians: The Secret Mapping of the New World.*

Picknett, Lynn and Prince, Clive. (1998) *The Templar Revelation: Secret Guardians of the True Identity of Christ.*

Picknett, Lynn and Prince, Clive. (2007) *The Turin Shroud: How Da Vinci Fooled History.*

Pinkham, Mark Amaru. (2004) *Guardians of the Holy Grail: The Knights Templar, John the Baptist, and the Water of Life.*

Read, Paul Piers. (1999) *The Templars.*

Robinson, John J. (1991) *Dungeon, Fire and Sword.*

Sora, Steven. (1999) *The Lost Treasure of the Knights Templar: Solving the Oak Island Mystery.*

Sora, Steven. (2004) *Lost Colony of the Templars: Verrazano's Secret Mission to America.*

Wallace-Murphy, Tim and Hopkins, Marilyn. (2007) *Templars in America.*

Wallace-Murphy, Tim. (2008) *The Knights of the Holy Grail: The Secret History of the Knights Templar*.

Young, John K. (2003) *Sacred Sites of the Knights Templar: Ancient Astronomers and Freemasons at Stonehenge, Rennes-le-Château and Santiago de Compostela*.

MEROVINGIANS

Baird, Robert Bruce. (2008) *Merovingians: Past and Present Masters*.

Gardner, Laurence. (2003) *Realm of the Ring Lords: The Myth and Magic of the Grail Quest*.

Geary, Patrick J. (1994) *Before France and Germany: The Creation and Transformation of the Merovingian World*.

Murray, Alexander Callander. (2000) *From Roman to Merovingian Gaul: A Reader*.

Murray, Alexander Callander. (2005) *Gregory of Tours: The Merovingians*.

Wallace-Hadrill, J. M. (1982) *The Long-Haired Kings and Other Studies in Frankish History.*

Wood, I. (1995) *The Merovingian Kingdoms, 450-751.*

METAPHYSICS AND SPIRITUALITY

Ambrose, Kala. (2007) *9 Life Altering Lessons: Secrets of the Mystery Schools Unveiled.*

Braden, Gregg. (1995) *Awakening to Zero Point: The Collective Initiation.*

Braden, Gregg. (1997) *Walking Between the Worlds: The Science of Compassion.*

Braden, Gregg. (2000) *The Isaiah Effect: Decoding the Lost Science of Prayer and Prophecy.*

Braden, Gregg. (2000) *Beyond Zero Point: The Journey to Compassion.*

Braden, Gregg, (2004) *The God Code: The Secret of Our Past, The Promise of Our Future.*

Braden, Gregg. (2004) *The Divine Name: Sounds of the God Code* (audio book).

Braden, Gregg. (2005) *The Lost Mode of Prayer* (audio CD).

Braden, Gregg. (2005) *Unleashing The Power of The God Code: The Mystery and Meaning of the Message in Our Cells* (audio CD).

Braden, Gregg. (2005) *An Ancient Magical Prayer: Insights from the Dead Sea Scrolls* (audio book).

Braden, Gregg. (2005) *Speaking the Lost Language of God: Awakening the Forgotten Wisdom of Prayer, Prophecy and the Dead Sea Scrolls* (audio book).

Braden, Gregg. (2005) *Awakening the Power of A Modern God: Unlock the Mystery and Healing of Your Spiritual DNA* (audio book).

Braden, Gregg. (2006) *Secrets of The Lost Mode of Prayer*.

Braden, Gregg. (2007) *The Divine Matrix: Bridging Time, Space, Miracles and Belief*.

Bunick, Nick. (1998) *In God's Truth.*

Chopra, Deepak. (1998) *The Path to Love: Spiritual Strategies for Healing.*

Chopra, Deepak. (2005) *Peace Is The Way: Bringing War and Violence to An End.*

Coelho, Paulo. (1998) *The Alchemist.*

Coelho, Paulo. (2003) *Warrior Of The Light.*

Cooper, Adrian P. (2008) *Science of Being In Twenty Seven Lessons.*

Crowley, Gary. (2006) *From Here to Here: Turning Toward Enlightenment.*

Das, Lama Surys. (1998) *Awakening the Buddha Within.*

Das, Lama Surys. (2000) *Awakening to the Sacred: Creating a Spiritual Life From Scratch.*

Das, Lama Surys. (2001) *Awakening the Buddhist Heart: Integrating Love, Meaning and Connection Into Every Part of Your Life.*

Das, Lama Surys. (2003) *Living Kindness: The Buddha's Ten Guiding Principles for a Blessed Life.*

Das, Lama Surys. (2003) *Letting Go of the Person You Used To Be: Lessons on Change, Loss and Spiritual Transformation.*

Doucette, Michele. (2010) *A Travel in Time to Grand Pré.* (second edition)

Doucette, Michele. (2010) *The Ultimate Enlightenment For 2012: All We Need Is Ourselves.*

Doucette, Michele. (2010) *Turn Off The TV: Turn On Your Mind.*

Doucette, Michele. (2010) *Veracity At Its Best.*

Doucette, Michele. (2011) *Sleepers Awaken: The Time Is Now To Consciously Create Your Own Reality.*

Doucette, Michele. (2011) *Healing the Planet and Ourselves: How To Raise Your Vibration.*

Doucette, Michele. (2011) *You Are Everything: Everything Is You.*

Doucette, Michele. (2011) *The Awakening of Humanity: A Foremost Necessity.*

Doucette, Michele. (2011) *The Cosmos of The Soul: A Spiritual Biography.*

Doucette, Michele. (2011) *Getting Out Of Our Own Way: Love Is The Only Answer.*

Doucette, Michele. (2012) *Living The Jedi Way.*

Doucette, Michele. (2012) *Vicarius Christi: The Vicar of Christ.*

Dyer, Wayne. (1998) *Manifest Your Destiny: The Nine Spiritual Principles For Getting Everything That You Want.*

Dyer, Wayne. (2002) *Getting in the Gap: Making Conscious Contact with God Through Meditation* (book and CD).

Ford. (2005) *Becoming God.*

Ford, Debbie. (2010) *The 21 Day Consciousness Cleanse: A Breakthrough Program for Connecting with Your Soul's Deepest Purpose.*

Freke, Timothy. (2005) *Lucid Living.*

Freke, Timothy. (2009) *How Long Is Now? A Journey to Enlightenment and Beyond.*

Freke, Timothy, and Gandy, Peter. (2001) *The Jesus Mysteries: Was the Original Jesus a Pagan God?*

Freke, Timothy, and Gandy, Peter. (2002) *Jesus and The Lost Goddess: The Secret Teachings of the Original Christians.*

Freke, Timothy, and Gandy, Peter. (2006) *The Laughing Jesus: Religious Lies and Gnostic Wisdom.*

Freke, Timothy, and Gandy, Peter. (2007) *The Gospel of the Second Coming.*

Gawain, Shakti. (1993) *Living In The Light: A Guide to Personal and Planetary Transformation.*

Gawain, Shakti. (1999) *The Four Levels of Healing.*

Gawain, Shakti. (2000) *The Path of Transformation: How Healing Ourselves Can Change The World.*

Gawain, Shakti. (2003) *Reflections in The Light: Daily Thoughts and Affirmations.*

Hansard, Christopher. (2003) *The Tibetan Art of Positive Thinking.*

Hicks, Esther and Hicks, Jerry. (2004) *Ask and It Is Given: Learning to Manifest Your Desires.*

Hicks, Esther and Hicks, Jerry. (2005) *The Amazing Power of Deliberate Intent: Living the Art of Allowing.*

Hicks, Esther and Hicks, Jerry. (2006) *The Law of Attraction: The Basics of the Teachings of Abraham.*

Hicks, Esther and Hicks, Jerry. (2008) *The Astonishing Power of Emotions: Let Your Feelings Be Your Guide.*

Hicks, Esther and Hicks, Jerry. (2009) *The Vortex: Where The Law of Attraction Assembles all Cooperative Relationships*

James, John. (2007) *The Great Field: Soul At Play In The Conscious Universe.*

Judd, Isha. (2008) *Why Walk When You Can Fly: Soar Beyond Your Fears and Love Yourself and Others Unconditionally.*

Katz, Jerry. (2007) *One: Essential Writings on Nonduality.*

Koven, Jean-Claude. (2004) *Going Deeper: How To Make Sense of Your Life When Your Life Makes No Sense.*

Kribbe, Pamela. (2008) *The Jeshua Channelings: Christ Consciousness in a New Era.*

Lama, Dalai. (2004) *The Wisdom of Forgiveness: Intimate Conversations and Journey.*

McTaggart, Lynne. (2003) *The Field: The Quest For The Secret Force Of The Universe.*

McTaggart, Lynne. (2008) *The Intention Experiment: Using Your Thoughts to Change Your Life and the World.*

McTaggart, Lynne. (2011) *The Bond: Connecting Through the Space Between Us.*

Millman, Dan. (1990) *Way of the Peaceful Warrior.*

Millman, Dan. (1991) *Sacred Journey of the Peaceful Warrior.*

Millman, Dan. (1992) *No Ordinary Moments: A Peaceful Warrior's Guide to Daily Life.*

Millman, Dan. (1995) *The Life You Were Born To Live.*

Millman, Dan. (1999) *Everyday Enlightenment.*

Moses, Jeffrey. (2002) *Oneness: Great Principles Shared By All Religions.*

Nichols, L. Joseph (2000) *The Soul As Healer: Lessons in Affirmation, Visualization and Inner Power.*

Peniel, Jon. (1998) *The Lost Teachings of Atlantis: The Children of The Law of One.*

Peniel, Jon. (1999) *The Golden Rule Workbook: A Manual for the New Millennium.*

Price, John Randolph. (1987) *The Superbeings.*

Price, John Randolph. (1998) *The Success Book.*

Quinn, Gary. (2003) *Experience Your Greatness: Give Yourself Permission To Live* (audio CD).

Radin, Dean I. (2006) *Entangled Minds: Extrasensory Experiences in a Quantum Reality.*

Radin, Dean I. (2009) *The Conscious Universe: The Scientific Truth of Psychic Phenomena.*

Rasha. (1998) *The Calling.*

Rasha. (2006) *Oneness.*

Redfield, James. (1995) *The Celestine Prophecy.*

Redfield, James. (1997) *The Celestine Vision: Living the New Spiritual Awareness.*

Redfield, James. (1998) *The Tenth Insight.*

Redfield, James. (1999) *The Secret of Shambhala.*

Renard, Gary. (2004) *The Disappearance of the Universe.*

Renard, Gary. (2006) *Your Immortal Reality: How To Break the Cycle of Birth and Death.*

Rennison, Susan Joy. (2008) *Tuning the Diamonds: Electromagnetism and Spiritual Evolution.*

Ruiz, Don Miguel. (1997) *The Four Agreements: A Practical Guide to Personal Freedom.*

Ruiz, Don Miguel. (1999) *The Mastery of Love: A Practical Guide to The Art of Relationship.*

Ruiz, Don Miguel. (2000) *The Four Agreements Companion Book.*

Ruiz, Don Miguel. (2004) *The Voice of Knowledge: A Practical Guide to Inner Peace.*

Ruiz, Don Miguel. (2009) *Fifth Agreement: A Practical Guide to Self-Mastery.*

Schuman, Helen. (1997) *A Course in Miracles.*

Schwartz, Robert. (2009) *Your Soul's Plan: Discovering the Real Meaning of the Life You Planned Before You Were Born.*

Sharma, Robin. (1997) *The Monk Who Sold His Ferrari.*

Sharma, Robin. (2005) *Big Ideas to Live Your Best Life: Discover Your Destiny.*

Shinn, Florence Scovel. (1989) *The Wisdom of Florence Scovel Shinn.*

Shinn, Florence Scovel. (1991) *The Game of Life Affirmation and Inspiration Cards: Positive Words For A Positive Life.*

Shinn, Florence Scovel. (2006) *The Game of Life* (book and CD).

Talbot, Michael. (1992) *The Holographic Universe.*

Talbot, Michael. (1993) *Mysticism and the New Physics.*

Tolle, Eckhart. (1999) *The Power of Now: A Guide to Spiritual Enlightenment.*

Tolle, Eckhart. (2001) *Practicing the Power of Now: Meditations, Exercises and Core Teachings for Living the Liberated Life.*

Tolle, Eckhart. (2001) *The Realization of Being: A Guide to Experiencing Your True Identity* (audio CD).

Tolle, Eckhart. (2003) *Stillness Speaks.*

Tolle, Eckhart. (2003) *Entering The Now* (audio CD).

Tolle, Eckhart. (2005) *A New Earth: Awakening to Your Life's Purpose.*

Twyman, James. (1998) *Emissary of Peace: A Vision of Light.*

Twyman, James. (2000) *The Secret of the Beloved Disciple.*

Twyman, James. (2000) *Portrait of the Master.*

Twyman, James. (2000) *Praying Peace: In Conversation with Gregg Braden and Doreen Virtue.*

Twyman, James. (2008) *The Moses Code: The Most Powerful Manifestation Tool in the History of the World.*

Twyman, James. (2009) *The Kabbalah Code: A True Adventure*.

Twyman, James. (2009) *The Proof: A 40-Day Program for Embodying Oneness*.

Vanzant, Iyanla. (2000) *Until Today*.

Virtue, Doreen. (1997) *The Lightworker's Way*.

Virtue, Doreen. (2006) *Divine Magic: The Seven Sacred Secrets of Manifestation* (book and CD).

Walker, Ethan III. (2003) *The Mystic Christ: The Light of Non-Duality and the Path of Love According to the Life and Teachings of Jesus*.

Walsch, Neale Donald. (1999) *Abundance and Right Livelihood: Applications for Living*.

Walsch, Neale Donald. (2000) *Bringers of The Light*.

Walsch, Neale Donald. (2002) *The New Revelations: A Conversation with God*.

Walters, J. Donald. (2000) *Awaken to Superconsciousness: How To Use Meditation for Inner Peace, Intuitive Guidance and Greater Awareness*.

Walters, J. Donald. (2000) *Meditations to Awaken Superconsciousness: Guided Meditations on The Light* (audio cassette).

Walters, J. Donald. (2003) *Meditation for Starters* (book and CD).

Walters, J. Donald. (2003) *Metaphysical Meditations* (audio CD).

Walters, J.Donald. (2003) *Secrets of Bringing Peace On Earth*.

Weisenthal, Simon. (1998) *The Sunflower: On the Possibilities and Limits of Forgiveness*

Weiss, Brian. (2001) *Messages From the Masters: Tapping Into The Power of Love*.

Weiss, Brian. (2002) *Meditation: Achieving Inner Peace and Tranquility in Your Life* (book and CD).

White, Mary Mageau. *Preparing for Ascension* e-book (an interactive study course).

White, Mary Mageau. *Our Chakra System: A Portal to Interdimensional Consciousness* e-book.

Wilcock, David. *The Shift of the Ages – Convergence Volume One* (online book) [315]

Wilcock, David. *The Science of Oneness – Convergence Volume Two* (online book) [316]

Wilcock, David. *The Divine Cosmos – Convergence Volume Three* (online book) [317]

Wilcock, David. *Wanderer Awakening: The Life Story of David Wilcock* (online book) [318]

---

[315] http://divinecosmos.com/start-here/books-free-online/18-the-shift-of-the-ages
[316] http://divinecosmos.com/start-here/books-free-online/19-the-science-of-oneness
[317] http://divinecosmos.com/start-here/books-free-online/20-the-divine-cosmos
[318] http://divinecosmos.com/start-here/books-free-online/25-wander-awakening-the-life-story-of-david-wilcock

Wilcock, David. *The Reincarnation of Edgar Cayce* (online book) [319]

Wilcock, David. *The End of Our Century* (online book edited by David Wilcock) [320]

Wilcock, David. (2011) *The Source Field Investigations: The Hidden Science and Lost Civilizations Behind the 2012 Prophecies.*

Williamson, Marianne. (1996) *A Return To Love.*

Williamson, Marianne. (1997) *Morning and Evening Meditations and Prayers.*

Williamson, Marianne. (2002) *Everyday Grace: Having Hope, Finding Forgiveness and Making Miracles.*

Williamson, Marianne. (2003) *Being In Light* (audio CD set).

---

[319] http://divinecosmos.com/start-here/books-free-online/22-the-reincarnation-of-edgar-cayce-draft-of-pt-1
[320] http://divinecosmos.com/start-here/books-free-online/26-the-end-of-our-century

Wolf, Fred Alan. (1989). *Taking the Quantum Leap: The New Physics for Nonscientists*.

Wolf, Fred Alan. (2000). *Mind Into Matter: A New Alchemy of Science and Spirit*.

Wolf, Fred Alan. (2002). *Matter Into Feeling: A New Alchemy of Science and Spirit*.

Wolf, Fred Alan. (2004). *The Yoga of Time Travel: How the Mind Can Defeat Time*.

Wolf, Myke. (2010). *Create from Being: Guide to Conscious Creation*.

Wuttunnee, Stéphane. *Dreaming the Pyramid* e-book.

Yogananda, Paramahansa. (1979) *Metaphysical Meditations: Universal Prayers, Affirmations and Visualizations*.

Yogananda, Paramahansa. (2004) *The Second Coming of Christ: The Resurrection of the Christ Within You*.

Zukav, Gary. (1998) *The Seat of The Soul*.

Zukav, Gary. (2001) *Thoughts from The Seat of The Soul: Meditations for Souls in Process*.

Zukav, Gary and Francis, Linda. (2001) *The Heart of The Soul: Emotional Awareness*.

Zukav, Gary and Francis, Linda. (2003) *The Mind of The Soul: Responsible Choice*.

Zukav, Gary and Francis, Linda. (2003) *Self-Empowerment Journal: A Companion to The Mind of The Soul: Responsible Choice*.

Zukav, Gary. (2010) *Spiritual Partnership: The Journey to Authentic Power*.

REINCARNATION

Semkiw, Walter. (2011) *Born Again: Reincarnation Cases Involving Evidence of Past Lives with Xenoglossy Cases Researched by Ian Stevenson*.

Shroder, Tom. (2001) *Old Souls: Compelling Evidence from Children Who Remember Past Lives*.

Stevenson, Ian Dr. (1997) *Where Reincarnation and Biology Intersect.*

Stevenson, Ian Dr. (1997) *Reincarnation and Biology: A Contribution to the Etiology of Birthmarks and Birth Defects.*

Stevenson, Ian Dr. (1980) *Twenty Cases Suggestive of Reincarnation.*

Stevenson, Ian Dr. (2000) *Children Who Remember Previous Lives: A Question of Reincarnation.*

Tucker, Jim. (2008) *Life Before Life: Children's Memories of Previous Lives.*

ADDITIONAL CATHAR RELATED WEBSITES

A Brief History of the Inquisition [321]

A Guide to the Occitan Language [322]

A History of Herbs for Herbalists, Part 1 [323]

Arnaud Amaury [324]

Béziers [325] [326]

Cassoulet [327]

---

[321]

http://www.ironmaidencommentary.com/?url=album10_xfactor/inquis
ition&lang=eng&link=albums

[322] http://occitanet.free.fr/en/index.html

[323] http://www.planetherbs.com/case-studies/a-history-of-herbalism-
for-herbalists-part-1-how-the-arabs-saved-greek-sciences.html

[324] http://www.cathar.info/120502_arnaud.htm

[325] http://en.wikipedia.org/wiki/B%C3%A9ziers

[326] http://artsymbol.wordpress.com/2011/04/07/beziers-with-the-rest-
of-the-gold-and-silver-that-he-brought-from-spain-he-constructed-
another-church-of-saint-james-in-the-city-of-beziers/

[327]

http://www.cliffordawright.com/caw/food/entries/display.php/topic_id
/8/id/104/

Castles and Chateaux of Old Navarre [328]

Cathar Castles [329]

Cathar Honour: Paratge [330]

Catharism [331]

Cathedral Saint-Nazaire in Béziers [332]

Château de Foix [333] [334] [335]

Cinnamon: One of the World's Oldest Healers [336]

Counts of Foix [337]

---

[328] http://www.kellscraft.com/Navarre/OldNavarreContentPage.html
[329] http://www.catharcastles.info/
[330] http://www.dhaxem.com/data/handt/Cathar_Honour.pdf
[331] http://en.wikipedia.org/wiki/Catharism
[332] http://www.sports-sante.com/index.php/visite-de-la-cathedrale-saint-nazaire-a-beziers-herault-languedoc-roussillon
[333] http://en.wikipedia.org/wiki/Ch%C3%A2teau_de_Foix
[334] http://en.wikipedia.org/wiki/File:Chateau_de_Foix.jpg
[335]
http://www.castlesandmanorhouses.com/catharcastles/foix.php?key=fo
ix
[336] http://self-help.vocaboly.com/archives/1114/cinnamon-one-of-the-worlds-oldest-healers/
[337] http://en.wikipedia.org/wiki/Counts_of_Foix

Danté and the Fedeil d'Amore [338]

Eastern Hemisphere 1100 AD (map) [339]

Esclarmonde de Foix [340] [341] [342]

Europe 1135 (map) [343]

Fennel: Medicinal Uses [344]

Foix [345]

Foix and Its Château [346]

Foix and Montségur [347]

---

[338] http://web.eecs.utk.edu/~mclennan/Classes/US310/Dante-Fedeli-d-Amore.html

[339] http://upload.wikimedia.org/wikipedia/commons/d/d0/East-Hem_1100ad.jpg

[340] http://www.cathar.info/120516_esclarmonde.htm

[341] http://www.rosicrucian.org/publications/digest/digest2_2011/04_web/09_hbernard/09_hbernard_112311.pdf

[342] http://en.wikipedia.org/wiki/Esclarmonde_of_Foix

[343] http://www.skyscrapercity.com/showthread.php?t=384050&page=8

[344] http://www.herbsarespecial.com.au/free-herb-information/fennel.html

[345] http://en.wikipedia.org/wiki/Foix

[346] http://www.kellscraft.com/Navarre/OldNavarreCh11.html

[347] http://www.art-science.com/Tourism/France/Cathars/c4.html

Foix Castle [348]

Gazetteer of Cathar Castles [349]

Herbs of Eastern Europe [350]

Historic Cities: Béziers [351]

Holly Lore [352]

Horrible Massacre at Béziers in Christ's Name [353]

House of Foix [354]

Hugh III, Duke of Burgundy [355]

La Madeleine and Mysticism [356]

---

[348] http://www.ariege.com/chateaudefoix/info.html
[349] http://shadowtheatre13.com/gazetteer.html
[350] http://www.gallowglass.org/jadwiga/herbs/easterneuropeherbs.html
[351] http://www.languedoc-france.info/030109_beziers.htm
[352] http://dutchie.org/holly-lore/
[353] http://www.christianity.com/ChurchHistory/11629815/
[354] http://en.wikipedia.org/wiki/County_of_Foix#House_of_Foix
[355] http://en.wikipedia.org/wiki/Hugh_III,_Duke_of_Burgundy
[356] http://www.panoccitania.com/mysticism.html

Lordship of L'Îsle-Jourdain [357]

Medicinal and Magical Herbs of Medieval Europe [358]

Medieval Herbs [359]

Myths and Legends about Herbs and Spices [360]

Occitan Alphabet [361]

Occitan Language [362]

Old Occitan [363] [364]

Old Occitan (French Dictionary) [365]

Paratge [366]

---

[357] http://en.wikipedia.org/wiki/Lordship_of_L%27Isle-Jourdain
[358] http://www.quantal.demon.co.uk/saga/ooc/herbs.html
[359] http://www.medieval-recipes.com/medievalgarden/herbs.htm
[360] http://www.ehow.com/about_5417655_myths-legends-herbs-spices.html
[361] http://en.wikipedia.org/wiki/Occitan_alphabet
[362] http://en.wikipedia.org/wiki/Occitan_language
[363] http://en.wikipedia.org/wiki/Old_Occitan
[364] http://www.lingweenie.org/occitan/
[365] http://lengadoc.chez.com/lexic_medieval.htm
[366] http://www.midi-france.info/190403_paratge.htm

Personal Seal of Roger IV of Foix (grandson of Raymond Roger) [367]

Phillip II of France [368]

Phillip II of France: Conflict with King Richard [369]

Pont Serme [370]

Raymond Roger de Foix [371]

Raymond Roger Trencavel [372]

Richard I of England [373]

River Orb viewed from Béziers [374]

---

[367] http://www.midi-france.info/191600_seals.htm

[368] http://en.wikipedia.org/wiki/Philip_II_of_France

[369] http://en.wikipedia.org/wiki/Philip_II_of_France#Conflict_with_King_Richard_1192.E2.80.931199

[370] http://en.wikipedia.org/wiki/Pont_Serme

[371] http://www.cathar.info/120514_foix.htm

[372] http://en.wikipedia.org/wiki/Raymond-Roger_of_Trencavel

[373] http://en.wikipedia.org/wiki/Richard_I_of_England

[374] http://en.wikipedia.org/wiki/File:River_Orb_viewed_from_Beziers.JPG

Roger Bernard I, Count of Foix [375]

Romance Languages [376]

Seige of Acre (1189 to 1191) [377]

Septimania [378]

Septamia in 537 (map) [379]

Song of the Albigensian Crusade [380]

The Arms of Foix [381]

The Cathars [382]

The Counts of Foix [383]

---

[375] http://en.wikipedia.org/wiki/Roger-Bernard_I_of_Foix
[376] http://en.wikipedia.org/wiki/Romance_language
[377]
http://en.wikipedia.org/wiki/Siege_of_Acre_(1189%E2%80%931191)
[378] http://en.wikipedia.org/wiki/Septimania
[379] http://en.wikipedia.org/wiki/File:537Septimania3.svg
[380] http://en.wikipedia.org/wiki/Song_of_the_Albigensian_Crusade
[381] http://www.cathar.info/120550_crusadersarms.htm#foix
[382] http://www.ancientquest.com/embark/cathars.html
[383] http://www.cathar.info/120514_foix.htm

Time Will Tell

The Counts of Toulouse and the Kings of England [384]

The Cult of the Saints [385]

The Duty to Paratge [386]

The Feminine Principle [387]

The Great Esclarmonde of the Cathars [388]

The Healing Properties of Herbs [389]

The History of the Languedoc – Romans: The Via Domitia [390]

The House of Toulouse [391]

---

[384] http://www.midi-france.info/190202_england.htm

[385] http://artsymbol.wordpress.com/category/the-cult-of-the-saints/

[386] http://joyofequivocating.blogspot.ca/2009/12/duty-to-paratge-maaht-natural-order.html#!/2009/12/duty-to-paratge-maaht-natural-order.html

[387] http://www.panoccitania.com/femaleprinciple.html

[388] http://www.dhaxem.com/data/handt/The_Great_Esclarmonde_of_the_Cathars.pdf

[389] http://www.labyrinth.net.au/~obsidian/bos-herbs1.html

[390] http://www.languedoc-france.info/100401_viadomitia.htm

[391] http://www.midi-france.info/1902_houseoftoulouse.htm

The House of Trencavel [392] [393] [394]

The Knights Templar [395]

The Kybalion Resource Page [396]

The Mysterious History of Occitania [397]

The Troubadors [398]

The White Lady [399]

Third Crusade [400]

Toulouse: Kings, Dukes and Counts [401]

---

[392] http://www.midi-france.info/1914_trencavel.htm
[393] http://en.wikipedia.org/wiki/House_of_Trencavel
[394] http://medievalwinter.blogspot.com/2009/06/house-of-trencavel.html
[395] http://www.panoccitania.com/templars.html
[396] http://www.kybalion.org/
[397] http://www.panoccitania.com/secrets.html
[398] http://www.languedoc-france.info/1904_troubadours.htm
[399] http://shadowtheatre13.com/whitelady.html
[400] http://en.wikipedia.org/wiki/Third_Crusade
[401] http://fmg.ac/Projects/MedLands/TOULOUSE.htm#_Toc225040405

---

[402] http://www.utm.edu/staff/globeg/occit.shtml

[403] http://www.trobar.org/troubadours/

[404]
http://www.bibliotecapleyades.net/ciencia/ciencia_tuathadedanaan.htm

[405]
http://www.bibliotecapleyades.net/merovingians/blueapples/blueapple
s_05.htm

[406] http://www.wisegeek.com/what-are-fava-beans.htm

[407] http://www.successconsciousness.com/affirmations_self_talk.htm

[408] http://www.successconsciousness.com/index_000008.htm

[409] http://www.successconsciousness.com/index_00000e.htm

How to Make a Vision Board [410]

How to Make a Vision Board [411]

Links to Creative Visualization Articles (Remez Sasson) [412]

Mind Movies [413]

The Power of Affirmations [414]

The Power of Repeated Thoughts and Words [415]

What Are Affirmations and How To Affirm [416]

HEALTHEOLOGIST

Healtheology [417]

---

[410] http://www.oprah.com/spirit/How-to-Make-a-Vision-Board-Find-Your-Life-Ambition-Martha-Beck
[411] http://christinekane.com/how-to-make-a-vision-board/
[412] http://www.successconsciousness.com/creative-visualization-articles.html
[413] http://www.mindmovies.com/?10107
[414] http://www.successconsciousness.com/index_00000a.htm
[415] http://www.successconsciousness.com/index_00004b.htm
[416] http://www.successconsciousness.com/affirmations.htm
[417] http://www.aiht.edu/catalog/healtheology.asp

Healtheology [418]

Need More Energy? [419]

LABYRINTHS

Build Your Own Labyrinth [420]

Directions to Make a Labyrinth [421]

How to Build a Simple, Prayer Journey [422]

Instructions for Creating a Simple Labyrinth [423]

Karen's String Labyrinths Page [424]

Labyrinthia [425]

---

[418] http://marcelainsignares.com/healthology.php
[419] http://www.overhall.com/body_work.htm
[420] http://www.lessons4living.com/build.htm
[421] http://labyrinthsociety.org/make-a-labyrinth
[422] http://www.nph.com/vcmedia/2369/2369464.pdf
[423] http://www.kpcc.com/laby_instructions.htm
[424] http://www.angelfire.com/my/zelime/labyrinthsstring.html
[425] http://www.labyrinthina.com/path.htm

Laying out a Labyrinth [426]

Rainbow Labyrinths [427]

The Chartres Cathedral Labyrinth [428]

METAPHYSICS

130 Principles of Metaphysics [429]

American Association of Drugless Practitioners School Listing [430]

Aristotle's Metaphysics [431]

Fundamental Principles of the Metaphysics of Morals [432]

Healing Humanity Network [433]

---

[426] http://www.labyrinthos.net/layout.html
[427] http://www.rainbow-labyrinths.co.za/create_your_own/index.html
[428] http://www.labyrinthos.net/chartresfaq.html
[429] http://forums.vsociety.net/index.php?topic=11158.0
[430] http://www.aadp.net/
[431] http://plato.stanford.edu/entries/aristotle-metaphysics/
[432] http://librivox.org/fundamental-principles-of-the-metaphysic-of-morals-by-immanuel-kant/
[433] http://humanityhealing.net/member-area/

Heart Intelligence [434]

Introduction to Metaphysics [435]

Laws of Metaphysics [436]

Man as Creator [437]

Metaphysical Bible Interpretation [438]

Metaphysical Center for Humanistic Science and Spirituality [439]

Metaphysical Science [440]

Metaphysical Works of Immanuel Kant [441]

Metaphysics [442]

---

[434] http://www.metaphysics-for-life.com/heart-intelligence.html
[435] http://www.phorrigan.fcpages.com/
[436] http://www.whatismetaphysics.com/laws-of-metaphysics.html
[437] http://www.som.org/7creator/move.htm
[438] http://www.divinemetaphysics.org/BibMetaTB.html
[439] http://www.mchschurch.org/
[440] http://www.metaphysics-for-life.com/metaphysical-science.html
[441] http://www.gutenberg.org/browse/authors/k#a1426
[442] http://en.wikipedia.org/wiki/Metaphysics

Metaphysics [443]

Metaphysics by Aristotle [444]

Metaphysics for Life Study Guide [445]

Metaphysics: Philosophy of Science [446]

Ontology [447]

Parmenides [448]

Principles of Spiritual Evolution, Part 1 [449]

Principles of Spiritual Evolution, Part 2 [450]

---

[443] http://plato.stanford.edu/entries/metaphysics/
[444] http://classics.mit.edu/Aristotle/metaphysics.html
[445] http://www.metaphysics-for-life.com/studyguide.html
[446] http://www.spaceandmotion.com/Metaphysics-Principles-Reality.htm
[447] http://en.wikipedia.org/wiki/Ontology
[448] http://en.wikipedia.org/wiki/Parmenides
[449] http://montalk.net/metaphys/42/principles-of-spiritual-evolution-part-i
[450] http://montalk.net/metaphys/43/principles-of-spiritual-evolution-part-ii

Seven Spiritual Practices [451]

Spiritual Metaphysics [452]

Teachings from Reverend Mario Schoenmaker: Metaphysics [453]

The Dark Night of the Soul [454]

The Definition of Metaphysics [455]

The History of Metaphysics [456]

The Metaphysical Elements of Ethics [457]

The Metaphysical Institute of Higher Learning [458]

---

[451] http://www.whatismetaphysics.com/seven-spiritual-principles.html
[452] http://www.metaphysics-for-life.com/spiritual-metaphysics.html
[453] http://www.ica.org.au/institute/documents-articles/Metaphysics-IM.pdf
[454] http://www.metaphysics-for-life.com/dark-night-of-the-soul.html
[455] http://www.metaphysics-for-life.com/definition-of-metaphysics.html
[456] http://www.metaphysics-for-life.com/history-of-metaphysics.html
[457]
http://www.marxists.org/reference/subject/ethics/kant/morals/ch01.htm
[458] http://metaphy.com/Semesters/semes1.html

The Metaphysics of Money [459]

The Mind Body Connection [460]

The Philosophy of Metaphysics [461]

The Theory of Knowledge [462]

What Becoming a Metaphysician Means [463]

What is a Metaphysician? [464]

What is Ontology? [465]

World Metaphysical Association [466]

What is Metaphysics? [467]

---

[459] http://www.metaphysics-for-life.com/donate.html
[460] http://www.metaphysics-for-life.com/mind-body-connection.html
[461] http://www.metaphysics-for-life.com/philosophy-of-metaphysics.html
[462] http://www.metaphysics-for-life.com/theory-of-knowledge.html
[463] http://www.som.org/7creator/move.htm
[464] http://www.catherinecollautt.com/blog/what-is-a-metaphysician/
[465] http://www.metaphysics-for-life.com/ontology.html
[466] http://www.worldmeta.org/
[467] http://www.metaphysics-for-life.com/what-is-metaphysics.html

METAPHYSICAL INSTITUTIONS

American Institute of Holistic Theology [468]

CanAm College: Education for the Healthy Mind [469]

IMU: International Metaphysical University [470]

International College of Metaphysical Theology [471]

The College of Divine Metaphysics [472]

The Institute of Transpersonal Psychology [473]

The School of Metaphysics [474]

University of Metaphysical Sciences [475]

------

[468] http://www.aiht.edu/
[469] http://www.innerpeaceawareness.com/Courses.html
[470] http://intermetu.com/
[471] http://www.metaphysicscollege.com/
[472] http://www.divinemetaphysics.org/PracMetaTB.html
[473] http://www.itp.edu/index.php
[474] http://www.schoolofmetaphysics.com/
[475]
http://www.umsonline.org/AllAboutMetaphysicalMetaphysics/Metaph
ysicalMetaphysicsCoursesWhatWillLearn.htm

University of Metaphysics [476]

University of Sedona [477]

ONLINE COURSES

All about Herbs [478]

Aromatherapy 101 [479]

Astrology 101 [480]

Auras [481]

Buddhism 101 [482]

Chakras 101 [483]

---

[476] http://www.metaphysics.com/
[477] http://www.universityofsedona.com/Metaphysical-University-Sedona-Metaphysics.htm
[478] http://www.universalclass.com/i/course/learn-about-herbs.htm
[479] http://www.universalclass.com/i/crn/30409.htm
[480] http://www.universalclass.com/i/crn/7550039.htm
[481] http://www.universalclass.com/i/course/how-to-interpret-auras.htm
[482] http://www.universalclass.com/i/course/buddhism-101.htm
[483] http://www.universalclass.com/i/crn/7550043.htm

Chakra Clearing [484]

Chakra Meditation 101 [485]

Cosmology 101 [486]

Crystal Therapy [487]

Energy Healing [488]

Flower Essences 101 [489]

Homeopathy 101 [490]

Life Coaching 101 [491]

Lifetime Wellness 101 [492]

---

[484] http://www.universalclass.com/i/course/chakra-clearing-class.htm
[485] http://www.universalclass.com/i/course/chakra-meditation-101.htm
[486] http://www.universalclass.com/i/course/cosmology_101.htm
[487] http://www.universalclass.com/i/course/learn-crystal-healing.htm
[488] http://www.universalclass.com/i/crn/31254.htm
[489] http://www.universalclass.com/i/course/learn-about-flower-essences.htm
[490] http://www.universalclass.com/i/course/learn-homeopathy-online.htm
[491] http://www.universalclass.com/i/course/life-coaching-101.htm
[492] http://www.universalclass.com/i/course/lifetime-wellness-101.htm

Massage 101 [493]

Meditation 101 [494]

Metaphysics 101 [495]

Numerology 101 [496]

Nutrition 101 [497]

Psychic Powers 101 [498]

Reflexology Basics [499]

Reiki 1st Degree [500]

Reiki 2nd Degree [501]

---

[493] http://www.universalclass.com/i/course/learn-massage-therapy-online.htm
[494] http://www.universalclass.com/i/course/meditation-101.htm
[495] http://www.universalclass.com/i/course/study-metaphysics-101.htm
[496] http://www.universalclass.com/i/crn/7550041.htm
[497] http://www.universalclass.com/i/course/nutrition-basics-101.htm
[498] http://www.universalclass.com/i/crn/7550042.htm
[499] http://www.universalclass.com/i/crn/30446.htm
[500] http://www.universalclass.com/i/course/study-reiki-first-degree.htm
[501] http://www.universalclass.com/i/course/study-reiki-second-degree.htm

Reiki Attunements [502]

Reiki Essentials [503]

Reiki Hand Placements [504]

Self Hypnosis 101 [505]

Spiritual Counseling 101 [506]

Tarot Cards 101 [507]

Teaching Reiki [508]

The Runes [509]

---

[502] http://www.universalclass.com/i/course/reiki-attunements-how-to.htm
[503] http://www.universalclass.com/i/course/understanding-reiki.htm
[504] http://www.universalclass.com/i/course/study-reiki-hand-placements.htm
[505] http://www.universalclass.com/i/course/self-hypnosis-101.htm
[506] http://www.universalclass.com/i/course/spiritual-counseling-101.htm
[507] http://www.universalclass.com/i/course/tarot-cards-how-to.htm
[508] http://www.universalclass.com/i/course/how-to-teach-reiki.htm
[509] http://www.universalclass.com/i/course/learn-how-to-use-runes.htm

Wellness Coaching 101 [510]

Wicca 101 [511]

World Religions 101 [512]

Yoga 101 [513]

PYRAMID INFORMATION

Bosnian Pyramid [514]

Pyramidal Water [515]

Pyramid Energy: Probing the Bovis Legend [516]

Pyramid of Life [517]

---

[510] http://www.universalclass.com/i/course/how-to-be-a-wellness-coach.htm
[511] http://www.universalclass.com/i/course/wiccan-study.htm
[512] http://www.universalclass.com/i/course/world-religions-101.htm
[513] http://www.universalclass.com/i/course/learn-yoga.htm
[514] http://www.bosnianpyramid.com/
[515] http://www.pyramidoflife.com/water.htm
[516]

http://www.skeptic.com/junior_skeptic/issue23/translation_Laigaard.html
[517] http://www.pyramidoflife.com/about.htm

Pyramid Power [518]

Pyramid Power [519]

Pyramids and Meditation [520]

Rods and the Pyramid [521]

Secrets of the Pyramids [522]

The Complete Pyramid Sourcebook [523]

The Great Pyramid, Lesson 3 [524]

The Healing House [525]

---

[518] http://www.earthbornerising.com/Pyramids.html
[519] http://www.iempowerself.com/84_pyramid_power.html
[520] http://www.kingdomcare.20m.com/custom.html
[521] http://www.egyptianhealingrods.com/rods-and-pyramid.html
[522] http://www.occulttreasures.com/secrets.html
[523]
http://sentinelkennels.com/GPimages/CompletePyramidSourcebook.pd
f
[524]
http://library.thinkquest.org/C0116484/english/simple/pyramid003.ht
m
[525] http://www.puresilica.com/glasspavilions/glasspavilions4.htm

---

[526] http://www.pyramid-cafe.in/Power.html
[527] http://www.world-pyramids.com/
[528] http://www.reversespins.com/singh.html
[529] http://www.coasttocoastam.com/show/2004/06/23
[530] http://www.childpastlives.org/childrenspastlives.htm
[531] http://www.reversespins.com/proofofreincarnation.html
[532] http://www.near-death.com/experiences/reincarnation01.html

IISIS: Institute for the Integration of Science, Intuition and Spirit [533]

Karma and Reincarnation [534]

Mellen-Thomas Benedict [535]

NDE: Arthur Yensen [536]

NDE: Dannion Brinkley [537]

NDE: David Perry (1762) [538]

NDE: Jeanie Dicus [539]

---

[533] http://www.iisis.net/index.php?page=reincarnation-evidence-past-lives-life-research-home&hl=en_US

[534] http://www.himalayanacademy.com/resources/pamphlets/KarmaReincarnation.html

[535] http://www.mellen-thomas.com/

[536] http://www.near-death.com/experiences/reincarnation06.html

[537] http://www.near-death.com/experiences/evidence11.html

[538] http://homepages.rootsweb.ancestry.com/~dagjones/docs/neardeath.html

[539] http://www.near-death.com/experiences/reincarnation05.html

NDE: Mellen-Thomas Benedict [540]

NDE: Thomas Sawyer [541]

Paul Gaugin and Peter Teekamp [542]

Reincarnation [543]

Reincarnation [544]

Reincarnation [545]

Reincarnation and the Early Christians [546]

Reincarnation and NDE Research [547]

Reincarnation Central [548]

---

[540] http://www.near-death.com/experiences/reincarnation04.html
[541] http://www.near-death.com/experiences/reincarnation03.html
[542] http://www.peterteekamp.com/summary.html
[543] http://www.blavatsky.net/topics/reincarnation/reincarnation.htm
[544] http://www.reincarnation2002.com/
[545] http://www.reincarnation.ws/
[546] http://www.near-death.com/experiences/origen06.html
[547] http://www.near-death.com/experiences/reincarnation02.html
[548] http://www.reincarnationcentral.com/sitemap.html

Reincarnation in Christian History [549]

Reincarnation: Its Meaning and Consequences [550]

Return of the Revolutionaries: The Case for Reincarnation and Soul Groups Reunited [551]

Scientific Proof of Reincarnation: Dr. Ian Stevenson's Life Work [552]

Statement of Reincarnation: Dalai Lama of Tibet [553]

Someone Else's Yesterday [554]

The Boy Who Lived Before [555]

The Michael Newton Institute: For Life Between Lives Hypnotherapy [556]

---

[549] http://www.near-death.com/experiences/origen08.html
[550] http://www.comparativereligion.com/reincarnation.html
[551] http://www.johnadams.net/
[552] http://reluctant-messenger.com/reincarnation-proof.htm
[553] http://dalailama.com/messages/tibet/reincarnation-statement
[554] http://www.confederateyankee.net/
[555] http://www.reversespins.com/The_Boy_Who_Lived_Before.html
[556] http://www.newtoninstitute.org/

The Question of Reincarnation, Part 1 [557]

The Question of Reincarnation, Part 2 [558]

The Question of Reincarnation, Part 3 [559]

The Reincarnation of Abraham Lincoln and John Fitzgerald Kennedy [560]

The Reincarnation Experiment: Paul Von Ward [561]

The Reincarnation of Jesus [562]

Wynn Free Interview: The Reincarnation of Edgar Cayce [563]

RUSSIAN NATIONAL ACADEMY OF SCIENCES

Introduction [564]

---

[557] http://www.fst.org/reinc1.htm
[558] http://www.fst.org/reinc2.htm
[559] http://www.fst.org/reinc3.htm
[560] http://www.near-death.com/experiences/reincarnation08.html
[561] http://www.reincarnationexperiment.org/
[562] http://www.near-death.com/experiences/origen04.html
[563] http://www.peopleyoushouldmeet.com/index.php/wynn-free
[564] http://www.gizapyramid.com/russian/introduction.htm

On The Way to Disclosing The Mysterious Power of The Great Pyramid [565]

Pyramid Powers Discovered by Ukraine and Russian Scientists [566]

Pyramid Research [567]

Pyramid Research [568]

SUBCONSCIOUS REPROGRAMMING

Canadian Association of Neuro Linguistic Programming [569]

I AM Wishes Fulfilled Meditation [570]

Meta NLP [571]

---

[565] http://www.gizapyramid.com/drv-article.htm
[566] http://abundanthope.net/pages/Environment_Science_69/Pyramid-Powers-Discovered-By-Ukraine-And-Russian-Scientists_printer.shtml
[567] http://www.gizapyramid.com/russian/research.htm
[568] http://www.egyptianhealingrods.com/pyramid-research.html
[569] http://www.canlp.ca/
[570] http://www.amazon.com/dp/1401937640/
[571] http://meta-nlp.co.uk/

Neuro Hypnotic Repatterning (NHR) [572]

Neiro Hypnotic Repatterning (NHR) [573]

Neuro Linguistic Programming (NLP) [574]

NLP Canada Training Inc. [575]

NLP Information Center [576]

Repatterning Hypnosis [577]

The Power of Practice [578]

The Secret of Deliberate Creation [579]

---

[572] http://www.neurohypnoticrepatterning.com/
[573] http://www.jonathanjenkyn.com/?p=80
[574] http://www.neurolinguisticprogramming.com/
[575] http://www.nlpcanada.com/
[576] http://www.nlpinfo.com/
[577] http://www.repatterninghypnosis.com/
[578] http://www.1shoppingcart.com/app/?Clk=2249883
[579] http://tinyurl.com/d2czud

Michele Doucette is webmistress of Portals of Spirit, a spirituality website whereby one will find links to [1] The Enlightened Scribe, [2] an ezine called Gateway To The Soul, [3] books of spiritual resonance as well as authors of metaphysical importance, [4] categories of interest from Angels to Zen, [5] up-to-date information as shared by a Quantum Healer, [6] affiliate programs and resources of personal significance, [7] healing resource advertisements and [8] spiritual news.

As a Level 2 Reiki Practitioner, she sends long distance Reiki to those who make the request, claiming only to be a facilitator of the Universal energy, meaning that it is up to the individual(s) in question to use these energies in order to heal themselves.

Having also acquired a Crystal Healing Practitioner diploma (Stonebridge College in the UK), she is guardian to many from the mineral kingdom.

She is the author of many spiritual/metaphysical works; namely, [1] *The Ultimate Enlightenment For 2012: All We Need Is Ourselves*, a book that was nominated for the AllBooks Review Best Inspirational Book of 2011, [2] *Turn Off The TV: Turn On Your Mind*, [3] *Veracity At Its Best*, [4] *The Collective: Essays on Reality* (a composition of essays in relation to the Matrix), [5] *Sleepers Awaken: The Time Is Now To Consciously Create Your Own Reality*, [6] *Healing the Planet and Ourselves: How To Raise Your Vibration*, [7] *You Are Everything: Everything Is You*, [8] *The Awakening of Humanity: A Foremost Necessity*, [9] *The Cosmos of The Soul: A Spiritual Biography*, [10] *Getting Out Of Our Own Way: Love Is The Only Answer*, [11] *Living The Jedi Way* and [12] *Vicarius Christi: The Vicar of Christ*, all of which have been published through St. Clair Publications.

In addition, she has written another volume that deals solely with crystals, aptly entitled *The Wisdom of Crystals*.

She is also the author of *A Travel in Time to Grand Pré*, a visionary metaphysical novel that historically ties the descendants of Yeshua (Jesus) to modern day Nova Scotia.

243

As shared by a reviewer, *Veracity At Its Best* "constructs the context for the spiritual message" imparted in *A Travel in Time to Grand Pré*.

Against the backdrop of 1754 Acadie, this novel, an alchemical tale of time travel, romance and intrigue, from Henry Sinclair to the Merovingians, from the Cathari treasure at Montségur to the Knights Templar, also blends French Acadian history with current DNA testing.

Together with the words of Yeshua as spoken at the height of his ministry, *A Travel in Time to Grand Pré* has the potential to inspire others; for it is herein that we learn how individuals can find their way, their truth(s), so as to live their lives to the fullest.

Several years in the making, she was also driven to write *Back Home With Evangeline*, the sequel to *A Travel in Time to Grand Pré*. It is here that Madeleine and Michel find themselves back in the twentieth century with a message that must be shared with the world. So, too, and even more importantly, must the message be lived, and experienced, by one and all.

When not working as a Special Education teacher, she continues to read, research and write, exploring her personal genealogies, all of which constitute her passion.

In the words of the Dalai Lama … *In order to be happy, one must first possess inner contentment; and inner contentment cannot come from having all we want; rather it comes from having and appreciating all we have.*

www.ingramcontent.com/pod-product-compliance
Lightning Source LLC
Chambersburg PA
CBHW060547260626
47161CB00003B/1087